CRY WOLF

SILVER HOLLOW COZY MYSTERY SERIES BOOK 4

LEIGHANN DOBBS

TRACI DOUGLASS

CHAPTER 1

No Trespassing! Violators Will Be Staked!

Silver Hollow Sheriff's Department Deputy DeeDee Clawson snorted at the makeshift sign as she walked toward the gates of the old Crenshaw property. It was bad enough she had to come out to this place to begin with. Ever since that fancy movie producer from Hollywood, Caine Hunter, had rented both the old Gothic-style mansion and the surrounding lands a few months back, she'd had one pain-in-the-butt complaint from townsfolk after another about the crowds and the noise and the weird people lurking about the set.

Not to mention all these pesky protestors.

Worse, though, was Caine Hunter himself. Always strutting around the small, picturesque downtown of Silver Hollow as if he owned the village—all slick West Coast glamour and movie-star handsomeness wrapped in a tight, muscular package of intrigue.

It was enough to give the average female werewolf fits.

Good thing DeeDee was far from average.

She patted the Taser clipped neatly to her utility belt and glanced at her partner for the day, Special Detective Dex Nolan. He was on loan to their department from the Federal Bureau of Paranormal Investigations—or FBPI. Over the past month or so, Dex had settled right in to life here in their beloved Silver Hollow.

The town was tiny and nestled in a gorgeous area of New Hampshire near the shores of a big lake in the White Mountains. Perfect for sightseeing or golfing in the summers—or all kinds of paranormal activities year round. In fact, Silver Hollow had one of the largest paranormal populations in the region. Witches, shifters, vampires—they had them all. Some folks said it was the remoteness of the town that made it so attractive to all the paranormals. After all, the closest big city was nearly a hundred miles away. Others said it was because of a magical current of power that came from all the surrounding nature. DeeDee, however, suspected the truth was simpler.

Paranormals like her loved Silver Hollow because it was a nice, quiet place to live.

Or at least it had been until Caine Hunter and his crew showed up.

A protestor wearing a knitted hat sporting two large red devil horns and carrying a homemade sign proclaiming DEMONS GO HOME bumped into DeeDee.

She gave the guy a dark stare. The protestor took one look at her expression and her Taser and scurried off fast.

Grrrr.

She shook her head and weaved through the crowds toward the perimeter of the Crenshaw property. They'd had a heck of a time even finding a place to park the squad car, having to nose through all the chaos without mowing down any unsuspecting rubberneckers or security guards.

"You about done with that phone call?" DeeDee asked Dex over her shoulder, narrowly avoiding another run-in with the horns guy.

Dex held up a finger and smiled. "Yeah, I know, Is. I love you too. Can't wait to see you later when I get home."

DeeDee managed to hold back a major eye roll—she was in uniform, after all—but just barely. One of the local witches, Issy Quinn, who owned a pet store called Enchanted Pets and was a good friend to DeeDee, had fallen madly, deeply, stupidly in love with Dex.

Not that DeeDee wasn't happy for them. They were both great people and deserved every bit of their happiness. If she were honest, though, she was a tad jealous. Issy and Dex were so perfect for each other, so attuned and affectionate, that their love seemed almost predestined.

She shook her head as Dex made kissing noises into his phone.

Ugh. Love.

Unfortunately, the only thing predestined in DeeDee right now was her arranged marriage to the new up-and-coming alpha of the neighboring MacPherson pack. It was a political move that had been arranged by her father when she was just a kid. With all the contracts and treaties signed and both packs depending on the merger to reinforce the truce between their two clans and increase their territories, there was no way DeeDee could get out of it now. The best she could hope for at this point was that this union wouldn't turn out to be the same awful disaster her own parents' contracted marriage had been.

It seemed that in werewolf pack politics, love was a luxury they couldn't afford.

Besides, if she didn't marry the son of the current MacPherson alpha, her own Clawson Pack Alpha father might make her younger sister do it, and that was unacceptable. DeeDee had learned her lesson long ago. She never shirked her duties or responsibilities.

Not after what had happened to poor Paige…

Shaking off the painful memories, she stopped at a set of huge rusted iron gates barring entry to the Gothic estate. Two beefy guards stood beneath a large sign with the movie's title.

The Vampire's Revenge.

More like the critics' revenge, once they got their hands on what would surely be the biggest flop of the season. DeeDee chuckled as she stepped up to one of the guards and flashed her badge. "Deputy Clawson, Silver

Hollow Sheriff's Department. This is my partner, Dex Nolan. We received a report of an incident involving injury on the set. We're here to investigate."

The guards exchanged a look then slowly creaked open the gates to let her and Dex inside. A group of protestors rushed forward to try and gain entry, but the guards pushed them aside. These women had on the same horned knitted hat as the other guy, but instead of carrying signs, they shouted all sorts of nasty insults and taunts toward the movie's cast and crew.

"Vamps are tramps!"

"Go back to hell where you came from!"

"Any world but Otherworld!"

Most people considered them a bunch of harmless extremist kooks, but DeeDee had checked out their website the day before at the office, during her lunch hour. The Sunrise Group's hate-filled rhetoric soon made her lose her appetite. They proclaimed themselves the harbingers of a brighter tomorrow but were truthfully the opposite of enlightenment. They detested all vampires and werewolves and any paranormal creature—basically anyone who wasn't exactly like them. From what she'd read, they were protesting Caine Hunter's movie because they didn't want the world of paranormals glorified.

Once she and Dex moved far enough away from the crowds, DeeDee sniffed the air, using her super-sensitive wolf senses. If those humans on the other side of the gate only knew how close they were to actual blood drinkers and shifters, a panicked riot would ensue.

Her sturdy winter boots crunched on the layer of snow blanketing the ground, and her new thick brown work coat kept her warm enough, despite the fact each breath DeeDee exhaled frosted on the air in front of her. Each time she inhaled, the slight chemical odor of the polyester fake fur still freaked her out a bit.

Honestly, she'd tried to get her boss, Owen Gleason, sheriff of Silver Hollow, to order the thing without the fake fur lining, but couldn't make too much of a fuss considering Owen knew zilch about the horde of paranormals living under his jurisdiction. In fact, Owen didn't even know creatures like her existed, thanks to DeeDee's effort to keep the truth hidden.

Normally, she kept the hood down, away from her face, for that reason. But today, her ears stung from the chill and the minus-zero wind chills, so she'd pulled the stupid thing up.

She and Dex headed around to the back of the property where a small group had huddled near the edge of a swampy woodland area. Lying near the center of the circle was a body. A very dead body, DeeDee surmised, given the two-foot-long stake protruding from the center of the corpse's chest.

"This looks like way more than an injury, Deputy," Dex said, wry amusement lacing his tone.

DeeDee gave him a thanks-for-stating-the-obvious stare then crouched beside the victim.

Sniffing again, she detected a faint whiff of garlic along with...

Uh-oh.

Nose scrunched, she straightened and looked around. Mistletoe.

With it being just a week until Christmas, she wasn't surprised to smell it, but that didn't stop her from hating it either.

Mistletoe held bad memories for her, and not just because she was allergic to the infernal stuff. First, there was all the kissing expected underneath it. Not that DeeDee had anything against kissing. It was just that right now, she had no one special to kiss. Sure, she'd dated a lot more since Gray Quinn, another local witch and Issy's cousin, had performed that midnight ritual on her to make her more attractive. Her friend Issy had tried to help her out too by giving DeeDee an acorn amulet to help bring out her "inner charms." But she still hadn't found anyone special. It was just as well—soon she'd be married.

A sneeze tickled her sinuses, and her arms started to itch like crazy beneath her jacket.

Yep. Mistletoe was the bane of her existence this time of year.

Despite her allergies, DeeDee continued to inspect the body as best she could with so many spectators still crowded around the scene. The victim's left hand appeared mangled, but there was no blood, indicating the wound had happened post-mortem.

She straightened and surveyed the area around the body. The damp ground had prevented the snow from sticking, so the dirt was easily visible. No footprints found, but there were several deep grooves leading away from where the body had been dumped.

Wheel marks? No, too narrow.

But maybe a sleigh, since the estate was quite large.

A hint of white protruded from the pocket of the victim's coat, and she bent to retrieve it. A napkin, from a local diner called The Coffee Connection. One side sported a coral-colored lipstick print.

"Right." DeeDee pulled out her cell phone and turned to Dex. "Can you secure the scene while I call it in?"

"Sure thing." Dex started moving people back from the body.

Fingers numb, DeeDee pulled off her gloves and punched in Owen's direct number then waited for two rings until he picked up.

"Sheriff Gleason."

"Hey, boss. It's DeeDee." She squinted over at a couple of girls flirting with Dex despite the fact that he was not reciprocating. Some gals were badge bunnies, no matter how impossible the odds. "We have a situation at the Crenshaw mansion."

"What kind of a situation?" Owen's voice perked up. Things had been a bit slow around Silver Hollow of late, and Owen always did love a good crime to solve.

"This injury is actually a murder."

"Yes!" Owen coughed to cover the excitement in his tone. "Oh. That's terrible. I'll call the ME and head over to the scene. You can never have too many eyes on the case."

"Right. See you soon, sir."

DeeDee ended the call then wandered back over to the crime scene. Dex had corralled all the movie people off to one side, a safe distance from the perimeter to prevent any further contamination of the site. Good. Contamination of a crime scene could lead to something being thrown out on a technicality, and every single shred of evidence was important to make a conviction. Another lesson learned from poor Paige. DeeDee wasn't about to make that same mistake, even if her hives were now getting so bad it felt as if her entire body were on fire.

To stay busy, and keep from scratching her skin raw, DeeDee walked back to their squad car and got a roll of tape and several posts out of the trunk to cordon off the area. She'd made it about halfway back to the crime scene when a young blond starlet rushed toward the body, screaming hysterically and crying. At least Dex managed to catch the woman before she flung herself atop the body.

DeeDee prayed for patience as she blocked off the area. After tying off the last section of tape, she turned and nearly stepped on the large smoke-gray cat sitting before her.

Brimstone. One of the many animal familiars to the Quinn witch cousins and a local Silver Hollow busybody. The feline stared up at her with his haughty hellfire-orange eyes and purred.

"What's the matter?" she asked him. "Cat got your tongue?"

Brimstone responded with a flat feline stare.

"Fine. Bad joke. Sorry." She stuffed what was left of the roll of tape into her pocket and stared down at the cat. He was plenty talkative when the Quinns were around, and she knew they frequently sent the cat out as a sort of drone spy to collect information for them. But DeeDee had never mastered the art of cat communication. So it was just meows and purrs and the occasional feline equivalent of an eye roll for her.

Today, though, Brimstone seemed to be trying to tell her something. He cocked his head toward the opposite side of the crime scene, meowing loudly. Then he paced —back and forth, back and forth—until finally DeeDee followed him.

About ten feet away, a fence lined the entire Crenshaw property. And sure enough, one section of chain link had a hole cut through the wire. Stuck on one side of the opening was a small swatch of sky-blue fabric flapping in the breeze.

DeeDee hurried to collect it in an evidence bag. Up close, she saw orange threads running through it too. "Good work, Brimstone."

The cat purred as if to say, "Of course," before sashaying away.

Sirens wailed louder as Owen arrived along with the ME's ambulance. Another car pulled up beside them—a black government-issue sedan. DeeDee's heart dropped as the driver emerged. Tall, skinny, dressed like a reject off the film *Men in Black* with his dark suit and aviator shades. Yep. It was Dex's boss at the FBPI, Stanley Judge.

Dex—despite his unfortunate employer, who tended to persecute paranormals more than serve, protect, and defend them—was a good man and friend to the creatures who lived in Silver Hollow. Heck, he'd even fallen in love with a witch.

But Stan? Well, Stan Judge was another matter entirely.

He seemed hell-bent on wrangling in any paranormals he could catch on his watch and shipping them off the FBPI's infamous Area 59, where all sorts of horrible experiments were done on the detainees, if the rumors were to be believed.

It was a good thing Stan wasn't the sharpest tack in the wall. DeeDee had kept him in the dark up until now about the paranormals in the area, and that had him convinced this movie set was nothing but make-believe.

The local medical examiner, Ursula Lavoie, climbed out of the driver's side of her ambulance and stalked up the drive alongside Stan. She looked stunning as always in a big white ermine coat with an enormous hood covering her face. Ursula was a vampire, so sunlight didn't agree with her, for obvious reasons. Funny thing, though—Ursula found Stan cute. Talk about opposites attracting. Although Stan *was* pasty white, which vamps seemed to like in a mate. And hey, if it got the creepy dude to quit ogling DeeDee, she was all for a romance between those two.

She met Owen and the others halfway up the drive and gave them a rundown of what she'd learned so far as they walked.

"Want me to start getting statements, boss?" she asked once they'd reached the crime scene again, hoping for a respite from the mistletoe. Several hard sneezes escaped her before she could stop them.

"Uh, sure, Deputy." Owen narrowed his gaze. "You aren't catching a cold, are you?"

"No. I'm fine. Just allergies, boss." DeeDee pulled out her trusty pad and pen then wandered over to pull spectators aside one by one. After interviewing people for about twenty minutes, however, she became a bit discouraged. No one seemed to have any idea what had happened to the victim. Which seemed particularly suspicious, given the trailers for the actors and crew lining the property. They were probably half a mile away, but still. Someone had to have heard something. Seriously. The victim had a stake driven through his heart. No way that would happen without a struggle or screaming.

DeeDee finished up with her last few people then met Ursula near the edge of the driveway where the body, now on a gurney, had been wheeled. "Explain to me how someone can die in such a brutal way and no one hears a thing."

"You mean the stake?" Ursula asked. "That's easy. It was driven through him post-mortem."

"He's not a vamp then?"

"Nope."

"So if the stake didn't kill him, what did?" DeeDee frowned.

"Not sure yet." Ursula signaled the EMTs to take the gurney to the ambulance. "I'll have to complete the autopsy to find that out."

"Right." Distracted, DeeDee waited until Ursula and the ambulance left, then wandered back toward the crime scene. Garlic, wooden stakes. All classic gear, yet no actual vampire killed. Deep in thought, she nearly ran into Stan, who stood staring at the scene, hands on his skinny hips.

"Don't you think this is odd?" he asked DeeDee.

She looked up and frowned. "What?"

"They're shooting a vampire movie, then some guy turns up dead with all the signs of being a vampire?" He gave DeeDee a side glance that raised her hackles. "Makes a guy wonder."

She bit back a sarcastic retort and looked away from Mr. Tall, Dark, and Dorky. "Yeah. Except there's no such thing as vampires."

"Maybe," Stan said as he strolled away toward the mansion.

Dex walked over to her next, his phone in hand again. This time, though, instead of talking to Issy, he was scrolling through stuff on the screen. "Check this out. Turns out the victim played the lead in the movie. He's an actor by the name of Tucker Rockwood." He showed her the screen. "You think maybe the killing's symbolic?"

"I don't know. Symbolic of what?"

"Maybe they were trying to prove a point?" He shrugged. "Perhaps one of the crazy protestors took things a step too far?"

"Could be." When DeeDee had interviewed the others, more than a few had said the victim had been something of a diva. They'd also said no one got along with Tucker and he was threatening to quit because of a contract dispute over more money. Given public interest was high in the film, despite its stupid title and outlandish plot, maybe the film's leading man had seen all the attention as a golden opportunity.

The crowds chanted in the distance as the ambulance pulled away. Owen was still with the crime scene techs, searching for any last bits of evidence, and she and Dex walked over to help them clear the area before returning to her squad car.

DeeDee had just gotten all the gear loaded into her trunk once more when an expensive Mercedes pulled in behind her cruiser, blocking her in. She scowled, ready to tell the driver to take a hike, when Caine Hunter emerged, along with a gorgeous, regal-looking blonde. He guided the woman by the elbow to where DeeDee stood behind her squad car.

"Deputy Clawson, always a pleasure to see you." Caine gave her a slight bow and a dazzling smile that made DeeDee's toes curl inside her boots. Darn him. It should be illegal for a man to look that hot at a crime scene. His warm amber gaze caught and held hers for a moment before he gestured toward the woman beside him. "This is my sister, Carletta."

"Deputy DeeDee Clawson. I work for Sheriff Gleason," she said, shaking the other woman's hand, feeling bulky and out of sorts next to such a delicate queen. Not that DeeDee was bad looking. She was okay, she supposed. Better now that Gray had given her a bit of a magical boost in the appearance department. Her curls bounced and sparkled despite the overcast day, her skin glowed with health and vitality, and her smile all but twinkled with whiteness. Still, under all the glitz and glamour, DeeDee still sometimes felt like the insecure tomboy she'd always been growing up, hardly worthy of standing in the presence of such beauty.

And yeah, Caine Hunter was beautiful, for a guy. All tall and broad and muscled, with his thick tawny-blond hair. Even his clothes—all designer, all cashmere, and all tailored to perfection—exuded the natural confidence and grace he seemed to carry with him wherever he went.

It wasn't fair. It was, in fact, downright annoying.

Maybe even more so today, because of all the red, itchy hives lurking beneath her drab brown work jacket. Not exactly cover-girl material or the kind of thing that made men beg to ask her out on a date. Not that she wanted to date Caine Hunter. Even if he did make her whole traitorous body light up like a Christmas tree whenever he was around.

Nope.

What she really needed was a good midnight run. They always helped tire out her inner wolf and clear her head and heart.

The only problem was, it was only midmorning at the latest. Plus, she now had a murder to investigate, and her number-one suspect was the guy standing before her now. Because, after all, if the top star of the movie had threatened to quit, who stood to lose the most if the film went under? Caine Hunter. That was who.

The same Caine Hunter whom DeeDee found inconveniently, impossibly attractive.

Not good.

Not good at all.

CHAPTER 2

*C*aine narrowed his gaze, trying to get a read on DeeDee. The few times they'd met since his arrival in Silver Hollow were under less than ideal conditions. Usually, the only time they saw each other was when she responded to a disturbance call on his movie set or to noise complaints from the neighboring homeowners. Which, given her slight frown and flat expression, hadn't exactly endeared him to her. And that made things...*difficult*.

Because DeeDee didn't know it yet, but Caine was her soon-to-be fiancé.

At least, that was his father's plan, and if Caine wanted to maintain his standing and approval within his pack, he was honor-bound to abide by his alpha father's wishes.

"She doesn't seem to like you," Carletta said, her tone

amused. "I think you'll have your work cut out for you this time, brother."

He snorted, watching as DeeDee crossed her arms over the top of that hideous brown coat. It was dull as dishwater and gave no indication of her shape underneath. Which was a shame, because his bride to be was quite pretty, beneath all her professional police procedures and bravado. Even in the deep chill, her thick golden curls shimmered, and her hazel eyes sparkled. Her skin was creamy, and her cheeks were flushed a delightful shade of pink from the cold. And her lips—soft and full and slightly tipped upward at the corners, as if she were constantly in on the joke—made him wonder how they'd feel against his mouth if he leaned in and kissed her.

Caine coughed to clear the sudden constriction from his throat. This was silly. He was marrying her because it was the right thing to do for his pack, because it was his duty as the heir apparent of the MacPherson alpha to seal the deal with the Clawsons and ensure no more wars would occur.

Still, as DeeDee continued to watch him, her booted toe tapping on the frozen ground and those delectable lips of hers pursed, he couldn't help thinking marriage to her might not be such a bad experience after all. The fact she responded to each of the calls about his property in a timely and thorough manner showed she was trustworthy and loyal and dedicated to justice. Plus, yeah. She was hot. Even as she glared at him across the few feet separating them. Perhaps her hostility toward him masked a stronger attraction. He called on his inner wolf senses and picked up clear pheromone signals and physical indications that might be the case—rising body temperature, increase in breath and pulse rate, pupils slightly dilated.

Good.

Physical attraction was a start. Now, they'd have to build on that and make their relationship into one tolerable for an eternity. Wolves mated for life, and werewolves like him and DeeDee, while not immortal, had a life expectancy far beyond human years—as long as they didn't meet with a silver bullet or another untimely demise.

Nope. Deal or not, when Caine took DeeDee for his bride, he wanted it to be far more than a business arrangement. He wanted a wife who would love him completely as a person, not for his money or for his family prestige or for his looks. But for him, the real Caine Hunter.

Transforming this contentious relationship from a battle of wills into a true partnership of respect and trust and love, however, would be tricky. Because right now, he had no doubt DeeDee saw herself as in charge—of this case and their upcoming engagement. And Caine was an alpha through and through, strong and tough and loyal and committed, born to lead. The last thing he wanted was to get into a power struggle with his as-yet-unaware new wife. But he also refused to sit back and let her and her department run roughshod over his movie set without keeping a close eye on them. His business depended on finishing and distributing this film.

"If you'll excuse me, Carletta." Caine moved to stand before his wife to be. "I'd like to see the crime scene, Deputy Clawson."

She raised a brow at him. "We're done collecting evidence."

"I'd still like to take a look." He grinned, the one that made most women fawn all over him. DeeDee just stared. No reaction. *Tough crowd.* Undeterred, Caine took off for the field behind her. "It's over here, correct?"

"You won't find anything," DeeDee said, rushing after him, her tone brimming with annoyance. "I never leave anything behind. Full, properly collected evidence means the difference between conviction and acquittal."

He stopped abruptly, and she nearly ran right over the top of him. Caine reached out a hand to steady her, but DeeDee pulled away before he touched her. He bit back a smile at her supremely irritated scowl. *I'm getting to her. Good.* In his experience, there was a fine line between love and hate. "Thanks for the law lesson, but I minored in criminal justice at Stanford."

"Really?" There went her crossed arms and tapping toe again. She looked adorable, but he refrained from saying so, thinking this would probably earn him a punch to the face. "Then you know how important it is to keep people from traipsing all over the crime scene."

"I do." He scanned the ground, picturing the way it had looked the day before when they'd shot scenes there.

He didn't have a photographic memory, but his was still sharper than the average person's. His wolf instincts helped too, honed from years of training by his father. He sniffed the air. "Is that garlic I smell?"

DeeDee's hazel eyes widened. "Yes. I smelled it too. Didn't find any on the victim or around the area, though. Figure someone must've ordered Italian food or something for lunch."

"Hmm." He walked the perimeter of the still-cordoned-off area then bent, squinting. "These marks are new. My crew and I shot footage here yesterday, but per our agreement to use this property, we always use plywood beneath our equipment to keep from tearing up the soil."

Her stony exterior fractured slightly as she moved in beside him. "I wondered about those when I saw them. Thought they could've been tire tracks, or maybe a sleigh."

"Those would have to be narrow tires, given the width of the marks left behind. I'd say a sleigh is more likely. Haven't seen one on the property, though." Caine looked up and found DeeDee's face only inches away. Her warm, minty breath fanned his skin, and her lips looked even more tempting from this close range. Her gaze flicked from his eyes to his mouth then back again, indicating he might not be the only one contemplating a kiss. And was that a gleam of respect he saw in her lovely gaze? Hope flickered anew inside him.

Then, as if realizing how near she was to him,

DeeDee blinked and frowned, backing away fast. "While your expert opinion is invaluable"—her sarcastic tone said the exact opposite—"the Silver Hollow Sheriff's Department has this under control."

Caine straightened and dusted off his hands as several minor actresses from the film flocked to his side, sobbing and clinging to him. In the past, he would've gone along with the situation. Actresses were attractive, after all, and eager for the attention—even though they were more interested in the size of his bank account than of his brains. But over the years, he'd had enough women climb into his bed because of family connections.

Now, he wanted a life mate who appreciated him for who he was inside.

"Well." He gently removed himself from the grasp of the sniffling girls who dampened the lapels of his cashmere coat, and headed back toward his Mercedes and his waiting sister. "I need to get back into town for a meeting."

DeeDee trailed behind him, silent, though he felt the weight of her stare tingling through his back. At the car, Caine turned and glanced at his soon-to-be spouse once more, giving her a curt nod. "Deputy."

"Mr. Hunter." DeeDee watched him as he climbed inside the car.

His sister slid into the backseat beside him then whispered, "Aren't you going to tell her?"

"Not yet. She'll find out soon enough who I am." Caine shrugged as the driver shut the door then jogged around the front of the car to climb behind the wheel. "Besides, when has telling the truth ever helped me in this business?"

Carletta sighed. "I was just thinking how awful it would be for her to hear it from the gossip mill. I know you've got trust issues after what happened with Brenda, but as a woman, I'd hate to find out who the man I'm going to marry is from a stranger."

Caine looked away, watching the image of DeeDee grow smaller in the side mirror as they pulled away. His sister was right. He did have trust issues. All because of Brenda, his first love way back in high school. She'd been everything he'd wanted—beautiful, popular, fun loving. He'd fallen head over heels, only to discover later the only reason Brenda had agreed to go out with him was because of his position in the MacPherson pack. It didn't help that she'd also cheated on him with the older alpha from another, competing pack. Since then, he'd closed off his heart. He never wanted to be betrayed like that again.

When his father had proposed an arranged marriage, Caine had thought it would be a safer alternative—all the benefits, none of the messy emotions. But given the way his body had just reacted around DeeDee today, the whole thing now seemed like a very bad idea. Yes, he was into her physically, but what if he'd read her wrong? The last thing he wanted was to be shackled to a woman who found him repugnant. And yeah, there'd been a few signs that maybe she didn't consider him completely hideous, but her defiant reactions led him to believe his union with her would be nothing but forced.

And forced was not what he wanted.

When the time came to admit to DeeDee who he truly was, Caine wanted DeeDee to agree to be his wife because she loved him, not because of some obligation to her pack. As much as it might rile his father's anger and put the peace between their packs at risk, if she truly didn't want to marry him, then he'd put measures into place to let her break the contract and their engagement. He wasn't a jerk, even if the reputation he'd cultivated in his wilder days said otherwise. Caine had grown over the years, matured, become a man he hoped one day would be worthy of pride and respect.

Not that he was ready to share that with anyone, not even Carletta.

Instead, he shrugged and settled back into his seat. "Don't worry about it. Or me. I can take care of myself."

CHAPTER 3

Once Caine's Mercedes turned at the end of the driveway, DeeDee found Owen and Dex huddled near the front of her cruiser.

"I'm heading back to the office," Owen told her as she walked up. "Need to notify the victim's next of kin. From what I found in the victim's wallet, he's married. Tucker and his wife rent a house down the street from here."

"I'll ride with you, if you don't mind," Dex said. "I want to pull some more of the victim's records from the FBI database and see if I can formulate a better motive for his murder. That might help us narrow down a list of suspects."

"I guess I'll stay here a bit longer then," DeeDee said, hunkering down inside her coat. "Maybe I can find out if anyone heard or saw anything suspicious."

"Fine." The guys gave her a brief wave then climbed into Owen's squad car and took off.

Great. DeeDee glanced around and saw Stan still lurking near the side of the house. Not exactly the partner of her dreams, but apparently all that was left since everyone else was gone. She headed over, pad and pen in hand, and stopped near where Stan was talking to one of the sniffling actresses who'd been draped all over Caine minutes earlier.

"Right, ma'am," Stan said, frowning. "I understand you thought Tucker Rockwood was hot. But did you ever see the victim go outside during the daytime?"

The brunette actress gave Stan a strange look then nodded.

"Huh, okay," Stan said. "What about noticing his reflection in a mirror?"

Yeah. That line of questioning would get them exactly nowhere. Any true paranormal knew better than to discuss their various "quirks" with humans. And Stan stood out like a sore thumb in that regard around here. She moved several feet away to question a redhead who'd all but stumbled over herself to get close to Caine. Shoving her biases aside, DeeDee forced a polite smile. "Do you have any idea who might have wanted Tucker Rockwood dead?"

The redhead dabbed her wet cheeks with a tissue then pointed toward the front gates of the mansion, where the knit-hatted protestors still milled about. "Why don't you ask them?"

After a few more minutes of unfruitful interrogations, DeeDee did exactly that, making her way down the drive and back to the Sunrise Group. Mr. Red Demon Horns made a beeline to her side and seemed eager to tell her anything she wanted to know. "Did you know Tucker Rockwood?"

"We knew of him, yeah," the guy said. "Not sorry to hear he's gone, either."

"Why's that?" DeeDee asked.

"He was a nasty piece of work, that guy was," the protestor said. "Used to stand here and yell insults at us all day long. Got so bad, Levi Harding stepped in and got into a shouting match with Rockwood. I thought those two would come to blows about it too, screaming at each other nose to nose."

"And who's Levi Harding?" DeeDee didn't look up as she furiously scribbled notes onto her pad.

"He's the leader of the Sunrise Group."

"Do you think this Mr. Harding held a grudge about his disagreement with Tucker Rockwood?"

"What?" The guy gave her a startled look. "Oh, no. I see where you're going with this, but there's no way Levi would've killed Rockwood. We don't want the vamps and werewolves dead—we just don't want them normalized or glorified, that's all."

She looked up at him, her gaze narrowed. "Where's your group staying while you're in town?"

"Over at the Route Nine Motel."

"Right." She jotted that down. Seedy place, over on the other side of Silver Hollow. She'd been called over there a couple months ago to solve another murder. Not exactly a five-star establishment. "Is Levi Harding here now?"

"Yep." The guy pointed toward a tough-looking dude near the side of the gates where the guards were stationed. He had on a black leather vest with a gray hoodie beneath it. No coat. Which was odd, given everyone else at the mansion was bundled up like Eskimos. Then again, some guys did dumb stuff like risk frostbite just to prove how manly they were. An image of Caine, all snug inside his thick cashmere coat, popped into her mind. He might be irritatingly gorgeous, but at least he had the common sense not to pull some dumb stunt like Easy Rider over there.

DeeDee made her way to Mr. Harding's side. "I'm Deputy DeeDee Clawson. Silver Hollow Sheriff's Department. Mind if I ask you a few questions?"

Levi gave a one-shoulder shrug, not meeting her eyes.

"Great," she said, flipping to a new blank page on her pad. "Can you tell me where you were last night, Mr. Harding?"

"After I left here at dusk, I went back to my motel."

"The Route Nine?"

"Yes, ma'am." He shifted slightly against the iron post, the toothpick sticking out of his mouth wobbling up and down as he chewed on it. "That's where all of us protestors usually go after a long day. A group of us went to eat at the little diner down the way from there, then we all went back to our rooms and went to bed."

"What time was that?"

28

"Early. About nine thirty. Why?"

"And you're sure everyone stayed in their rooms the rest of the night, Mr. Harding?"

"Yeah." He wrinkled his nose and finally looked up at her, his expression reminding her of an angry bulldog. "Where else would we go?"

"Good question." From his cagey demeanor, she suspected he was lying. "Thanks for your cooperation, Mr. Harding."

She flipped her pad closed and walked back to her cruiser, making a mental note to question Levi Harding again later.

CHAPTER 4

*L*ater that afternoon, DeeDee walked back into the office to find Owen hanging mistletoe over the door. She sidestepped around it, and Stan—who tried to trap her under it.

Ewww.

"What's the matter?" Owen called as she walked to her desk in the corner. "Don't want to get kissed?"

"I'm allergic," she said, tugging off her coat then hanging it on the nearby rack.

"To kissing?" Owen joked.

"To mistletoe." DeeDee gave her boss a look as she took her seat. "Gives me hives and makes me sneeze."

Dex strolled in and smiled at her. "Hey. Owen and I stopped at the house the Rockwoods are renting on the way back here."

"Yeah?" she said. "How'd the widow take the news of her husband's death?"

"Not well," Dex said. "She's still in shock, I think. Poor thing didn't know how to react when we told her, just kind of slumped there on her sofa."

"Didn't that seem a bit odd to you, though?" Owen climbed down from the ladder and dusted his hands off on his pants. Never one to wear a uniform, Owen was dressed today as he always was—khaki pants and a loud-printed Hawaiian shirt. "There were no tears. Nothing. Especially after she said she didn't even realize her husband hadn't come home for the night."

"Really?" DeeDee frowned. "That does sound strange."

"Not really." Dex sat back and stretched out his long legs. "Movies are a funny business. I remember one time when I lived in Ohio, some big-budget flick was getting shot near where I worked at the time. I had a day off, so I went out to the set to watch. Couple of the crew I talked to said it wasn't unusual for them to work all night sometimes. I'd suspect this movie's no different."

"That's true." Owen nodded. "Plus, she did say when Tucker worked late, he'd sleep in the den, which is downstairs from their bedroom. So, I guess it's conceivable she wouldn't know he was missing until she got up the next day. Even then, maybe she thought he'd gone in early or something."

"Okay," DeeDee conceded. "But I still wouldn't rule her out entirely yet. Spouses are always suspect number one in a murder investigation, right, boss?"

"Right." Owen walked back to his desk. "And Tucker

made a lot of money from his acting. Which his widow would stand to inherit if he passed away." He sat down then propped his feet up on his desk. "Let's give her a little time to process her husband's death, then we can go back tomorrow and talk to her again. What'd you find out from the rest of those protestors?"

"Not much," Stan said. He propped his hip on the corner of Dex's desk. "All of them said the cast and crew were out in the daylight and could see themselves in mirrors."

Owen gave DeeDee a what-the-heck glance, and she quickly took over the conversation. What was up with Stan? He wasn't even hiding the fact that he was here looking for paranormals.

"All the protestors are staying over at the Route Nine Motel during their time here in Silver Hollow. Talked to their leader too. Guy named Levi Harding. He seems like a real piece of work, but I'm not sure he's a killer. I'd still bet good money he was lying about where he was last night, though," she said. "He got all shifty when I asked him about his location."

"Huh." Dex rubbed his chin. "So we've got the widow and these crazy protestors for suspects."

"There's also Caine Hunter, the movie's producer-director," DeeDee added. "A couple of the crew told me Tucker Rockwood demanded more money for his role in the film and threatened to quit if he didn't get it. That would put Caine in a tough position financially."

"I still swear there's more going on out at that

mansion," Stan said, scowling. "My instincts went haywire on that property, and I'm never wrong when I sense parano—"

"Sure. Why don't you tell me more about it while we get something to drink?" Dex pushed out of his chair and grabbed Stan by the arm, pulling him toward the exit. Sometimes it was easier than others to keep the town's secrets from Owen. Dex patted Stan on the back as he escorted him out into the hall. "Vending machines are this way, Stan. My treat."

"That guy's squirrelly, isn't he?" Owen said, grinning. "Typical Fed."

"Yeah." DeeDee stood. "I'm going to run to the restroom. Be right back."

She headed down the hall to where Dex stood while Stan made his selection from the machine. She talked softly so Stan couldn't hear. "Your partner there thinks this has to do with paranormals, but I'm not sure it does. Do you think you can keep Stan the Man distracted long enough for us to figure it out?"

Dex smiled. "I'll do my best, Deputy. You really think this has no paranormal connection at all?"

"Not sure," she said.

"Hey, guys." Owen came down the hall toward them. "Ursula called. She's got some preliminary results on the victim. Want to head over?"

"Yep." DeeDee and Dex followed Owen back to the office, with Stan trailing behind them.

CHAPTER 5

*D*eeDee pushed through the double doors in the basement of Silver Hollow General Hospital and spotted Ursula across the room. It would be hard to miss her. Those bright-purple scrubs all but glowed beneath the harsh fluorescent lights overhead.

Her jet-black hair had been pulled back tightly into a bun, emphasizing her flawless pale skin and ruby-red lips. Stan nearly walked into the wall, he was so transfixed by the gorgeous ME. Luckily, DeeDee managed to redirect him in time as he stumbled past her and headed directly for the undead medical examiner. For a guy who was so intent on capturing a paranormal, he seemed clueless when actually faced with one.

DeeDee and Dex exchanged a here-we-go-again look, and she bit back a smirk.

Owen, being Owen, went about his business, totally unaware of the situation. He stood off to the side, flipping through the pages of Ursula's preliminary toxicology report and going over the tiny evidence bags she'd collected during Tucker Rockwood's preliminary examination.

Stan reached the table where the body was laid out and pretended to look the victim over, though anybody with eyes in their head could see his attention was fixed on Ursula the whole time. Every so often, she'd glance up from the instruments she was cleaning and give him a guarded stare.

"Did you find anything abnormal during your initial exam of the body?" Stan finally managed to ask, his voice oddly high and squeaky.

Ursula paused, a scalpel glinting between her fingers. "No."

Pressure built inside DeeDee's head, then a tickle—
a... a... A-CHOO!

Her sneeze echoed loudly in the tile room, and she held up a hand in apology. "So sorry. Excuse me."

Two more sneezes and another bout of scratching followed, though not as bad as at the film set. There must've been more mistletoe around or traces of it left on Tucker's clothes. She grabbed some tissues from a box on the counter and did her best to keep her scratching to a minimum. "What do those reports say, boss?"

Owen looked up from the papers as if just now realizing there were other people in the room. He cleared his throat, a slight frown knitting his brows. "Let's see. Tucker was forty-five. Time of death occurred around two a.m., but Ursula can't say exactly when the staking occurred until after the full autopsy's complete. From the amount of blood pooled on the left side of the body, it appears Mr. Rockwood's corpse had been in that position for quite some time after death. The body was then moved at some point, as evidenced by the fact the victim was found on his back. Again, no exact time for the transfer."

"Any idea what the actual cause of death was then?" DeeDee asked.

"Says here it was liver failure."

"Liver failure?" Dex asked.

"Yep. The early toxicology reports show he was poisoned by a combination of two substances—phoratoxin and phosphorus."

"Phosphorus?" Stan tore his gaze from Ursula to glance at Owen. "As in baking soda?"

"There are other substances containing phosphorus," Ursula said, her voice as smooth as silk. DeeDee could see how vamps lulled their victims into a hypnotic daze. As a werewolf, she was immune, but poor Stan looked ready to drop to his knees where he stood.

The medical examiner put down the last of her sparkling-clean instruments and came around the table to stand near Owen, who also seemed suspiciously immune to her undead charms. "Phosphorus can also be found in things like rat poison, fertilizers, fireworks, pesticides, and some household cleaners. Baking soda is fine in small doses, but if you ingest too much, it will kill you. It would have to be a heck of a lot, though, and our victim didn't have enough of it in his stomach."

"Huh," Owen said, his attention still focused on the reports. "What about this other chemical? I've never heard of a phoratoxin."

"Ah. I bet you have, you just didn't know it." Ursula winked over at DeeDee. "Phoratoxins come from plants. The one involved in this murder was Phoradendron tomentosum. Otherwise known as mistletoe."

As if on cue, DeeDee sneezed again.

Owen glanced up at her. "You going to be okay there, Deputy?"

She nodded from behind her tissue.

"Why would our killer use these two particular chemicals together?" Owen asked Ursula.

"Not sure. Perhaps they weren't sure how effective one would be alone, so they doubled up on the poison as insurance."

"So Rockwood was poisoned," Stan said, slowly moving around the table to where Ursula stood. "Then moved and staked through the heart. Takes a lot of force to drive something through the human body like that. I doubt Rockwood's wife would have enough strength." He frowned. "Unless she was a paranormal."

"I doubt that," DeeDee said, hoping to cut that train of thought off at the knees. She shot Dex a quick back-me-up-here look.

"I doubt there was anything like that involved, Detective Judge." Ursula narrowed her gaze on Stan. "The stake wasn't lodged deeply into the chest cavity. In fact, I'd say anyone with a mallet and a whole lot of anger could've done it."

Dex stepped forward, turning to DeeDee. "What about the lipstick-stained napkin you found in the victim's pocket? When Owen and I talked to the widow, she didn't look like the type to go for anything bright coral. Maybe Tucker had a girlfriend on the side."

"And if his wife found out, I doubt that would sit well with her," DeeDee said, brainstorming their new list of suspects.

"Any idea when the poison was ingested?" Owen asked.

"Unfortunately, no." Ursula crossed her arms, shoving her ample breasts higher. Stan's eyes nearly bulged out of his head. DeeDee bit back a laugh. Enthralled or not, the guy obviously had it bad for their medical examiner. "Since there's no way to tell exactly what time the body was moved, whoever gave it to him could've administered it earlier then left him to die. So they might have an alibi for the exact time of death. They could even have put it in food they knew he would eat later."

DeeDee cringed. "That's going to make it tough to verify alibis."

Owen set the reports aside. "Well, at least we know whoever murdered Rockwood would need access to the chemicals Ursula mentioned. My guess would be rat poison or a garden pesticide, since those would be the easiest to obtain without drawing suspicion. They'd also need a stake and the means to move a body."

"Movie sets usually have a prop room," Dex said. "Saw those too on that set I visited back in Ohio."

"Great." DeeDee moved toward the door, eager to get some fresh air and away from all that dreaded mistletoe. "I'll head back to the film set first thing in the morning and check it out. See if someone logged out a wooden stake and didn't return it."

CHAPTER 6

*A*s she walked into her home that night, DeeDee couldn't stop her brain from conjuring up images of Caine Hunter. She shrugged out of her bulky coat and tugged off her boots then walked into her log cabin's small but well-appointed kitchen. Most werewolf shifters she knew kept their homes on the smaller side and cozy, like modern versions of their age-old favorite den.

Not to say she didn't have all the amenities. In fact, she'd had this cabin custom-built in the woods just outside Silver Hollow a few years back, once she'd made deputy at the department. The job title came with a hefty pay raise, and she'd grown her nest egg large enough to afford the down payment on her first home.

The walls and cathedral-style ceiling in the living room were made of warm yellow pine, and the darker, stained oak floors gleamed beneath the recessed lighting. There was a huge outdoor patio in the back and a deck, which she sat out on at night and watched the stars or howled at the moon, depending on the time of the month. Her favorite part of the tiny house, though, was the huge stone fireplace. On cold winter nights, DeeDee loved to put on her flannel PJ's, grab her latest embroidery project and a mug of hot tea, and snuggle beneath her blanket in her comfy chair before the crackling flames. She'd also filled her house with sturdy, neo-rustic-style furniture, big enough and strong enough to withstand the weight of a full-grown werewolf—and her husband, whenever he arrived.

She made her way up to her bedroom in the loft and passed by the California King-sized bed. That was her second-favorite spot in the house. She'd spent lots of time picking out the perfect mattress then covered it with comfortable sheets and a snuggly down comforter. A plethora of pillows were strewn near the carved oak headboard, and four mighty wooden posts at each corner made her feel both protected and decadent.

She changed out of her uniform. Instead of PJ's tonight, though, she chose sweats. Excess energy and stress from the day still buzzed through her system. She needed to burn off some of it, or she'd never get to sleep tonight. After using the bathroom, DeeDee secured her brownish-auburn curls into a messy ponytail at the base of her neck then pulled on her running shoes and an extra navy-blue sweatshirt stamped with the words "Silver Hollow Police Academy" across the front in white. A run would be just the thing to drain her adrenaline.

Normally, she'd shift into her wolf form and go, but she also planned to stop by Issy Quinn's place on the other side of the lake and see if the Quinn cousins knew anything about the Rockwood murder. They always seemed to be in the loop, and considering Brimstone's appearance at the movie set earlier, she figured this time would be no exception.

Shifting, though, meant no clothes allowed. And since DeeDee wasn't in the mood to flash anyone tonight, having already used the secret stash of clothes she kept near Issy's place without replacing them yet, jogging as a human tonight was the only alternative.

After locking up her house, she set off down the lane toward the main road that led back into Silver Hollow proper. Whenever she took her runs, DeeDee was careful to stick to known territory. Venturing into the south side of town, especially at night, could be hazardous to one's health. Mainly because the South Side Witches lived there and were known to put strange curses and spells on visitors who dared to cross into their territory. The warnings were meant to deter other witches from entering their lands, but sometimes werewolves got caught in the hexes too.

The brisk cold felt good against her heated cheeks,

and DeeDee picked up her pace, her breath huffing out and frosting as she ran. With the holidays just around the corner, many of the houses lining the street were bedecked with lights and decorations. Being single, DeeDee didn't do much for the holidays around her place. She had a small Charlie Brownish-looking tree in the middle of her dining room table, and that was about it. When she'd been a kid, though, her parents had gone all out for her and her younger sister, Nia.

As she swerved onto the lane leading to Issy's home in the hills surrounding the lake, her memories turned nostalgic. Her mom had always been a sucker for Christmas, and her warm, caring spirit always made the holidays sparkle. Of course, that was before DeeDee had discovered just how awful her dad treated her mom.

Even now, five years on from her mother's death, it still made her blood boil.

Near her heart rested the pendant her mother had given her that last day. It was a mustard seed, encased in a tiny glass bubble. The seed, her mom told her, had the power to make someone change their mind or "plant a seed of an idea." She'd given it to DeeDee to help her avoid the same situation she'd ended up in—a loveless marriage.

Except there was no way DeeDee could escape the arrangement her father had made. Not without dire consequences for her younger sister. Nia was also the reason DeeDee had to go through with this marriage, no matter how she felt about her yet-to-be-revealed fiancé.

Because if DeeDee didn't marry this guy, chances were good their father would force Nia to do it.

She couldn't allow that to happen to her beloved sister.

So she'd go through with it. She would.

Now, if only her dad would get back from his honeymoon with his new—and much younger—wife so DeeDee could get the dumb ceremony over with, she'd be all set.

At the base of the foothills leading up into the mountains, she decided to veer off onto one of her favorite woodland paths, and before long, she came to the Promising Tree—a gnarled old pine tree, its trunk scarred from the claws of werewolves who'd come to promise their true love. Despite being an evergreen, the poor thing had precious few pine needles on it. Legend said when true love was promised, new leaves would flourish.

Will I ever stand here and pledge my true love?

Given she was marrying a stranger to seal a pack treaty, chances weren't good. Sighing, DeeDee turned away and spotted two sets of snowshoe prints through the moonlight. It was time to hit Issy's house. She sprinted the rest of the short distance to her friend's house then up the steps to the front door, knocking twice while she caught her breath.

Issy answered with a warm smile. "Hey, DeeDee. How are you? Come on in."

The Quinns were friendly, smart, hardworking—and a pretty talented bunch of witches to boot. She stepped inside Issy's house, and the place looked like a page out of a holiday magazine. White lights twinkled in every window, and a plain wreath with a red bow decorated the door.

"I didn't hear your car," Issy said as she closed the door behind DeeDee.

"Oh, I didn't drive." She gestured toward her running gear. "Needed to burn off some energy."

"Well, come sit by the fire then and warm up." Issy led her into the living room. The place smelled like pine and apple pie. Cheery carols played on the stereo. A cozy fire crackled in the fireplace, and a gorgeously decorated tree stood before the picture window looking out over the lake, and snow-capped mountains rose in the distance.

It all looked like something off a postcard.

From the large wraparound leather sofa, the three other Quinn cousins waved and greeted her—Raine, Ember, and Gray. Dex sat in an armchair across from them, a glass of eggnog in his hand. He gave DeeDee a brief wave.

Issy offered her some eggnog too, which DeeDee accepted, then she moved to take a seat next to Gray on the sofa. Before she could reach him, though, another sneezing jag happened. Sniffling, DeeDee looked up through watering eyes to see a sprig of mistletoe dangling from the entrance to the living room. Jeez, the offending stuff was everywhere these days.

Gray held out a box of tissues and patted the seat beside him. "Cold?"

"Allergies." She took a few tissues from the box then settled in.

"I might have some mistletoe varieties that wouldn't set off your sneezing," Raine offered. She ran the local greenhouse and was a specialist when it came to plants. "If you're interested."

"I'm not," DeeDee said, smiling. "But thanks anyway."

"So what brings you out tonight?" Issy asked, handing DeeDee her eggnog then taking a seat on the arm of Dex's chair. He slid his arm around her waist, and for a moment DeeDee felt a twinge of yearning. She'd love to have such easy affection with someone someday.

"Oh, like I told Issy, I was jogging and thought I'd stop by and say hello." She took a sip of her eggnog and found it heavy on the rum. Very tasty, but best to swig cautiously. No wonder Dex was over there grinning widely. He was probably feeling no pain at that point.

"And here I thought you'd come by to see if we knew anything about Tucker Rockwood," Ember said, winking. Ember ran the local chocolate shop, Divine Cravings. DeeDee was a frequent customer of the establishment. They had the best caramel pecan turtles ever.

"Well, now that you bring it up." DeeDee laughed along with the group, wishing her own family got along as well as the Quinns. "Did Dex fill you guys in on what happened?"

"Yep," Issy said. "Too bad we don't really know anything more than you do at this point. We'll keep our eyes out, though, and let you know if we see anything."

"Thanks."

"I told them about Stan's new obsession with Ursula too," Dex said.

DeeDee rolled her eyes. No need to contain it here, amongst friends. "Yeah. The only good thing is he's leaving me alone now."

"That *is* good," Issy said, chuckling. "He seemed to have the hots for you for a while."

She didn't miss the flicker of pity across Issy's face. The Quinn cousins knew all about her impending arranged marriage into the MacPherson pack and why it was so important she go through with it.

"I felt bad for Ursula, though," Dex said. "So much so that I volunteered to go back there tomorrow to get the final reports instead of Stan. And you know how badly that place creeps me out."

"You're a good man, buddy." DeeDee meant it too. Dex Nolan was the best, for a human. If only she could find a werewolf guy like him. Too bad her husband had been selected for her already. No sense mooning over that now, though. It was a done deal. "So you guys haven't seen or heard anything about possible paranormal involvement in the murder? I thought maybe since Brimstone showed up at the crime scene earlier, you guys had sent him."

"Nope," Raine said.

"Nothing here either," Ember agreed.

Gray just shook his head, unusually somber. He ran the local hair salon, Sheer Magic, and had all the women of Silver Hollow fawning at his feet. At six-foot-plus, his handsome, pirate-y good looks and sinful smile were the stuff of female dreams. He was always the charming life of the party too. So for her good friend to be so quiet and reserved took DeeDee aback.

"Well, that's good," she said, keeping her eye on Gray. "It means Owen can investigate to his heart's content and I don't have to worry about covering anyone's paranormal tracks for him or Stan."

They chatted for a while about the upcoming holidays, and Raine launched into a whole spiel about the pagan origins of the traditional Christmas tree. As interesting as it was, DeeDee couldn't help worrying about her friend, though.

"You okay?" she asked Gray quietly, nudging him with her shoulder. After all his help performing that full-moon ceremony to boost her attractiveness, DeeDee owed Gray big time. If he needed a friend, she was more than happy to return the favor. "Anything I can help with?"

"Nah." He seemed to give himself a mental shake and flashed her his dazzling smile. "Thanks, but I'm okay."

"Well, the offer stands. If you ever need anything, even just to talk, you let me know."

"Will do."

With that, DeeDee finished her eggnog then pushed

to her feet. "Well, Quinns, it's been super nice, but I have an early day tomorrow, so I'm going to head home."

"Want me to give you a ride?" Raine asked.

"Nope. The run will do me good." DeeDee waved on her way back to the door. "I'll let myself out. Everyone have a great rest of your evening."

CHAPTER 7

*a*n hour later, DeeDee was back at home, freshly showered and snuggled in her flannel PJ's, ready to relax and settle in with her favorite hobby—embroidery. She'd started doing it when she was a kid, making smaller pieces like handkerchief borders and napkin monograms then moving into bigger, more ambitious projects as the years went by.

Her latest endeavor was a large, intricate design of an appaloosa horse. The only real problem she had was once she started working on it, she lost all track of time. She'd look up and it would be eight p.m. Then the next time she checked the clock, four hours had somehow passed without her noticing. It had always been that way, unfortunately. Like when she was twelve and her mom had asked DeeDee to go to the corner store to get milk and—

"Ouch!" Distracted, she'd stuck herself in the finger with her needle. She frowned and stuck the tip of her index finger in her mouth. She'd been distracted the night of her mom's request too. Distracted by the embroidery project she'd been working on, the one she didn't want to take a break from to run to the store. So she'd talked Paige into going for her instead. Her cousin had been more than happy to get out of the house. She was always so energetic, so fun, so full of energy and life.

Until she'd been killed by a drunk driver on her way back from the grocery.

And it was all DeeDee's fault.

Sure, no one had come out and said they blamed her for the accident, but deep down, she knew the truth. Her distraction had caused Paige's death.

That kind of guilt took more than a lifetime to wash away.

To make matters even worse, the drunk who'd killed Paige had gotten off on a technicality because the police department had improperly handled the evidence in the case. That was the other reason DeeDee was so dedicated to her job now, why she worked so hard and so diligently to guarantee all the evidence was collected properly and recorded per regulations. She might not be able to bring her cousin back from the grave, but she sure as heck could make sure no one else got off on a technicality. Not on her watch, anyway.

She grabbed a tissue from the box on the end table and dabbed a small dot of blood off the end of her index finger. She'd just finished when her cell phone rang, and she answered without checking the caller ID. "Hello?"

"Hey, sis. It's Nia."

"Hey, girl. What's up?" DeeDee set her embroidery aside and curled her legs beneath her. Talking to her sister always helped to chase away the ghosts of her past. "How was your day?"

"Good. How about yours?"

"Okay. Working on a new murder case," DeeDee said. "So that's keeping me busy and out of trouble."

"Glad to hear it," Nia joked. They called each other at least three times a week to talk and were as close as any two siblings could be. "You're going to be a married woman soon," her sister said. "You better put your troubled days behind you."

"Yeah." DeeDee frowned and picked at a piece of nonexistent lint on the front of her shirt. "Have you talked to Dad lately?"

"No. Not since he left for his honeymoon," Nia said. "Why?"

"I don't know." She sighed and rested her head back against the chair, eyes closed. "I'm just eager to get this whole arranged marriage out of the way. And I haven't even met my future husband yet. I've tried calling Dad to find out specifics about the guy, but he's not answering his phone."

"Dad's on his honeymoon, sis." Nia snorted. "Can you blame him?"

"No, I guess not." DeeDee shook her head. "Plus, he's in the middle of nowhere, so I'm sure the cell reception isn't great either. Too bad none of that helps unravel the nervous knots in my stomach."

"Aw, don't be nervous, sis. I'm sure everything will work out just fine."

"That makes one of us then." She exhaled slowly. "It's just that I don't know squat about this guy I'm supposed to marry, Nia. The only info I have is he's the oldest son of the current alpha of the MacPherson pack and we're getting married to combine our territories."

"Okay," Nia said. "Well, if he's the oldest son, then that means he'll be alpha one day too, right? Which will make you the most powerful female in the new combined pack. Doesn't sound too bad to me."

"Yeah, but what if he's an idiot or he's mean or he's hideous looking? Or what if he thinks *I'm* those things?"

Her younger sister's laughter brightened DeeDee's somber mood. She knew she was probably overreacting, but sometimes just voicing her fears out loud helped dissipate some of her stress.

"I think it's almost worse *not* knowing," DeeDee continued. "I mean, by now I should've at least gotten an introduction to the guy, don't you think? Man, I wish Mom were here. She always knew the right thing to say to make me feel better."

"I know." Nia's voice turned wistful. "I miss her too. Dad's new wife is closer to our age than his, and she's trying to be more of a friend than a parental figure. I'm glad she's not trying to replace Mom, but it's just a different vibe."

"Yeah," DeeDee said. "Listen, I'm sorry, sis. I didn't mean to dump all my anxiety on you."

"Don't be silly. That's what sisters are for. Besides, you know you don't have to submit to this arranged marriage. There are ways out of it. The last thing I'd ever wish for you is a loveless marriage like Mom and Dad's."

"I can't refuse, Nia." Though it was a nice thought. "I'd be ostracized from the pack."

"Not necessarily."

"Seriously? Think about it, sis." DeeDee straightened in her seat. "It's true. If I so much as mentioned I had second thoughts about this whole thing, Dad would have a conniption fit, and you know the pack rules. If I outright refused, the pack could cut me out forever." DeeDee's heart twisted at the thought of never talking to her cousins, her pack friends, her father, and especially her sister again. That would be a fate worse than death. Worse than marrying a mean, hideous werewolf even.

"There's always the mustard-seed locket Mom gave you."

DeeDee clutched her necklace, wishing it were true but knowing in her heart it was probably just an old wolves' tale. And, honestly, even if there was some truth to the old legend, there was no guarantee it would work for her situation anyway. Years had passed since her mother had given her the locket, and even more time had gone by since the tiny reddish-brown seed had been sealed inside its glass bubble. For all DeeDee knew, the thing's idea-planting power had vanished long ago. Even if she planted the idea, it could backfire in so many ways. Then there was the fact she'd need the help of a super-powerful witch to unlock the whole spell anyway. And yes, she knew several of those, but that didn't mean any of the Quinns would even agree to help her.

"You still there, sis?" Nia asked.

"Yep. Sorry. Just thinking."

"About Mom?" her sister asked.

DeeDee squeezed her eyes shut as more painful memories rushed back. Her beloved mother's shrunken body, decimated by cancer. Her mom's clawlike hand reaching out, shaking, handing her the locket. That had been the day before she'd lapsed into the coma that finally took her life.

Against her palm, the mustard seed pendant warmed.

Perhaps there might be some magical juice left in it after all.

"Look," Nia said. "I'm not saying you should rush to any decisions. All I'm saying is you have the pendant for a backup plan, if you need it. You could smash the pendant and have a witch cast the spell to change Dad's mind about forcing the marriage. If the pack thinks it's his idea, then you won't face any adverse consequences."

"Maybe. I don't know." The only problem with Nia's plan was if DeeDee somehow got out of the arrangement, chances were good their father would simply move on to Nia and she'd get forced into the same marriage contract.

The only other person with the authority to call off the marriage was the MacPherson pack alpha. But again, even if by some small miracle that occurred, it would only free DeeDee from the prospect of an arranged marriage. Nia would still be prime pickings to unite their packs and forge a blood treaty to keep both their territories safe and secure.

Love never factored into these situations. It was all about politics.

Paige had died because DeeDee shirked her responsibilities, and she wasn't about to risk her little sister's life and happiness that way. Nia was younger and more sheltered, so she might not realize the ramifications of what she'd suggested.

Nope. She'd go through with the marriage because it was her duty, as her father's daughter and a member of the Clawson pack. No more discussion or wishing otherwise.

DeeDee forced a smile and changed the subject to Nia's favorite—shopping. "Find any bargains lately?"

"Heck yeah. Drove into Burlington yesterday and went on a massive splurge spree." As Nia chattered on about her new shoes and handbags, the world slowly returned to normal, and by the time the call ended, she and Nia were back on familiar, happier footing.

"I need to go, sis," DeeDee said. "Pulling an early shift in the department tomorrow."

"No problem. Go catch us some killers," Nia said, her warm smile evident in her voice. "Love you, sis."

"Love you too."

After switching off her phone, DeeDee tried to get

back into her embroidery again, but her heart just wasn't in it tonight. So she stowed her stuff back in the basket by the chair then got out her laptop to check her emails instead. Once those were sorted, she entered the embroidery chat room she liked to frequent, happy to see her favorite poster—Threads99—was also online. They'd begun an online friendship a few weeks earlier, bonding over their shared love of needlework and difficult projects. Plus, Threads99 was usually the only person in the chat room when DeeDee got in there—either late at night or early in the morning, when she couldn't sleep or woke up at four a.m. as she had several times this week.

It seemed Threads99 was a night owl too.

"Hey," her online friend typed into the message box. "Good to see you again. Just finished a new project."

A picture popped up on DeeDee's screen of a gorgeous woodland scene. The shading, the perfect stitching technique, the nuanced color palette—it took her breath away.

"I love it!" she typed back.

"Thanks," Threads99 responded. "What are you working on now?"

"Still my appaloosa." She spread out her work and took a quick photo with her phone, which she uploaded to the site for her online friend to see.

"Not much progress tonight," she typed. "Too much going on."

"Wow! That's sensational!" Threads99 typed back. "Nothing bad going on, I hope."

Her fingers hesitated over the keyboard. She knew Threads99 from the chat room, but that was about it. And while whoever was behind the moniker seemed nice, she was wary about sharing personal information with them. After all, she didn't know if Threads99 was male, female, wolf, or human. And yeah, maybe Threads99 was the closest thing DeeDee had to a best friend. That didn't mean she planned to go overboard with personal stuff. Yes, she liked chatting and exchanging pictures of their work, but deep inside, the thought niggled. How pathetic had her life gotten that the only new connection she'd formed with someone in ages was with a nameless, faceless person in an online chat room?

CHAPTER 8

*A*t work the next morning, DeeDee trudged up the driveway to the Crenshaw mansion. From all the lights and equipment ahead, it appeared filming was once again underway. She snorted. *Guess these Hollywood types don't let some pesky murder stand in their way.*

DeeDee flashed her badge to one of the guards near the gates, taking a quick glance around at the crowd still gathered. The protestors were still there, today boasting matching armbands to mark themselves as part of their group. It looked as if someone had thought to bring a large thermos of coffee as well. Many stood huddled together around it, their hands wrapped around steaming cups. They all had on matching dark jackets today too. It seemed the Sunrise Group became more organized each day.

She'd just passed through the gates and headed

toward the props trailer around the back of the property to check for any missing stakes when gunfire rang out.

Acting on pure instinct and training, DeeDee pulled her own weapon then crouched near the corner of the mansion. Her gaze darted right, then left, in search of the gunman. But when she looked at the movie set, no one had taken cover. All the actors walked around as though shots hadn't been fired.

What the—

Slowly, weapon still drawn, DeeDee straightened and shouted, "Get down! Gunfire!"

Several of the crew turned to look at her then laughed.

One of them yelled, "That's not gunfire. It's pyrotechnics. You know, fireworks? We use them for the sound and visual effects."

Heat clawed up from beneath DeeDee's uniform collar. *Right.* She clicked the safety back on and stowed her weapon back in its holster. She should've known everything around here was fake and frivolous.

Grumbling, she continued toward the props trailer, parked at the back of the house.

The thing was way bigger than she'd expected—more the size of a doublewide and ran the length of two semitrucks. She walked up the ramp to the inside and found a huge mess. Stuff scattered everywhere, with no rhyme or reason DeeDee could discern. In the far corner stood a petite Fae of indeterminate gender who looked equally disorganized, with their shirt on inside out and bright-green hair going every direction.

"Uh, I'm Deputy DeeDee Clawson with the Silver Hollow Sheriff's Department," she said to the Fae, showing her badge again. "I'd like to ask you a few questions, if that's okay?"

The props person squinted at her badge then shrugged. "Sure. What do you need?"

"I'm looking for stakes. Do you have any of those around here?"

"Duh. What kind of stakes? We got wooden, metal..." Props went flying as the person dug through a nearby pile of stuff. "Even found a cement one the other day." As proof, the Fae held the thing up. "This what you want?"

"The wooden ones, actually." DeeDee wrinkled her nose against the distinct odor of mustiness and garlic in the air. In fact, several large ropes of garlic cloves hung on the wall nearby. She guessed that explained where the smell around the body had come from. It was a movie about vampires, after all, so that made sense. Still, it was a wonder the props master could find anything at all in here. "What other kinds of things do you keep here?"

"Anything the crew might need," the Fae said. "Garlic, silver bullets, coffins, crucifixes. We got 'em all."

"How about mistletoe?"

The Fae's shoulders drooped a bit. "Nope. None of that."

"Okay." DeeDee pulled out her trusty notebook and

jotted down a few notes then peered through the piles and piles of crap surrounding her. Finally, she pointed toward the far corner. "Those look like wooden stakes. Mind if I take a look at those?"

"Go ahead." The Fae led her over.

Sure enough, they were just like the one used on Tucker Rockwood. She picked up one and inspected it. "Do you use a sign-out sheet when someone takes something from here?"

"Yes." The Fae zipped back through the piles then returned a moment later with a clipboard. "All props are to be signed out upon removal then signed back in again when they're returned."

DeeDee flipped through several pages of signatures, but no one had checked out a wooden stake. Not that she'd expected the killer to make things easy for them, but still. Best to cross all the T's and dot all the I's. She handed the clipboard back to the props master. "Is this trailer locked up at night to keep it secure?"

"There's a standard lock on the door, but we don't have any high-dollar items, so the production company isn't too concerned about stolen inventory."

"Right." DeeDee made a few more notes, mainly that the place was basically open to anyone able to pick a basic lock and with motive to murder. Finally, she slid her notebook and pen back into the pocket of her brown coat and walked to one corner of the trailer, noticing an abundance of dust bunnies and crud. "Do you guys ever have a problem with vermin? Rats or mice, specifically?"

"No." The Fae frowned. "Why?"

"So no need for rat poison in here?"

"Nope."

"Okay then. Thanks for your time." DeeDee stepped outside again, taking a deep breath of fresh air and glad for the open spaces. Being inside the trailer had felt too claustrophobic for her liking. While she stood at the bottom of the ramp, a woman came up to her. Based on her scent and her overabundance of fluttering layers of silky clothing, DeeDee pegged her as a witch.

"Are you investigating the murder?" the woman asked, holding out her hand. "I'm Sheila. I'm in charge of costumes for the film. I also do all the makeup and hair."

"Deputy Clawson, Silver Hollow Sheriff's Department." Following standard procedure, she shook the woman's hand then flashed her badge again. No way would a potential witness get away with not testifying because DeeDee didn't notify them of who and what she was. "Were you acquainted with Tucker Rockwood?"

As Sheila went on to describe in detail how well she knew the victim, DeeDee pulled out her notepad again. Oh, yeah, this gal was definitely a witch. And a drama queen, given the way she gestured wildly with her hands as she talked and her magically perfect makeup. There were times she envied the Quinns and their kin for their enchanted good looks, always perfect no matter what. But then again, no other paranormals besides werewolf shifters had the same connection to the forest and the land, so she supposed it all evened out in the end. Even if her hair still went wild sometimes, despite Gray Quinn's beauty spell.

Magic would only go so far, after all.

DeeDee scribbled her notes, focusing on Sheila's statement once more. "So you were pretty tight with Tucker Rockwood then?"

"Oh, sure. I get to know most of the cast, since I see them every day in my chair to do their makeup and hair. And all those fittings for the costumes. You see the real person during those times. A sort of intimate bond forms. They feel you're a friend, like they can tell you things they wouldn't normally tell other people. Lots of gossip."

"Gossip, eh?" DeeDee looked up from her paper. "And did Tucker tell you his secrets?"

"Well," Sheila said, her voice dropping to a whisper as she stepped closer to DeeDee. "He had a girlfriend. One of the other actresses. He never told me her name, but he said she was pretty, young, and blond."

That helped not at all. From what DeeDee could see, at least half a dozen girls running around the set fit that description. She turned back to Sheila. "Do you see anyone here who might be a candidate?"

Sheila gazed out over the set then shook her head. "Not really. Sorry. I'm sure that wasn't much help, but that's all I know. I swear."

"Okay. Thanks for your information." DeeDee waved as she headed for the gate, thinking about Rockwood's widow and the napkin with the lipstick stain. It was time to talk with the widow.

CHAPTER 9

On the way to Rockwood's rented home down the street from the Crenshaw property, DeeDee checked in with Owen via the squad car's onboard wireless Bluetooth. "Hey, boss. Wanted to let you know I checked out the props trailer. They had wooden stakes like the one used on the victim, but no record of who might've checked it out."

"Figures," Owen said. "You find out anything else?"

"Yes. I talked to the costume lady, and she said Tucker had a girlfriend. I'm heading back to talk to the widow again now."

"Great." The sound of shuffling papers echoed through the line. "I talked to Rockwood's lawyer right before you called. He said the wife stands to inherit everything, including collecting on her husband's two-million-dollar life insurance policy."

"Sounds like motive for murder." DeeDee pulled up to

the curb in front of the rented home. It wasn't nearly as large as the Crenshaw place but still huge and luxurious. She cut the engine and clicked open her seat belt.

"Sure does," Owen said. "Be careful, Deputy."

"Will do, sir." DeeDee ended the call then headed up to the front door.

Laura Rockwood answered on her third knock. She looked a bit less shell-shocked than DeeDee expected after what Owen and Dex had described the day before. From what she could tell, the woman was in her midforties but had aged well, her face unlined and her hair thick and dark brown.

No lipstick, DeeDee noticed. She made her standard introductory spiel, including badge.

"What can I do for you today, Officer?" Laura Rockwood asked, leaning against the doorframe.

"I'm sorry to bother you again, ma'am. But I'd like to ask you a few more questions, if you have a moment."

Laura gestured for DeeDee to come inside then closed the door behind her before leading her into a tastefully decorated living room filled with beige tones and lots of natural wood trim. "Would you like some coffee or water?"

"No, ma'am. I'm fine. Thanks." DeeDee took a seat on a leather sofa that most likely cost more than her entire house. "I'm sorry again for your loss."

"Thank you." Laura took a seat across from her in a stylish leather wing chair. "What else would you like to ask me about?"

"Right." DeeDee pulled out her notebook again, a tad disconcerted at how much the widow seemed to have recovered from her grief in one day. Yesterday, Owen and Dex had described her as overwrought and in shock at the loss of her husband. Today, she seemed sad and restrained but otherwise fine. DeeDee flipped back to the notes she'd taken from her colleagues' interview with the widow the day before. "You told the officers yesterday that you weren't concerned when your husband didn't come home Tuesday night. Why was that again?"

"Well, as I said, they do a lot of shooting at night on these horror films, so I was used to Tucker coming home at all kinds of odd hours. As I said to the other officers, when he did come home in the middle of the night like that, Tucker usually slept down here in the den to avoid waking me." Laura clasped her hands in her lap. "So when he didn't come home the other night, I assumed it was because things had run late again on the set." Laura's lips turned downward into a frown that didn't mar her Botox-injected forehead. "It wasn't until I didn't see him the next morning that I started to worry. But even then, I just assumed he'd gone back to the set early and that he'd call me later to check in."

"Okay." DeeDee jotted down the information. "Do you know anyone who might want your husband dead?"

Laura shrugged. "Tucker was the kind of outspoken guy who tended to rub some people the wrong way. I don't know anyone who disliked him enough to kill him, though."

While she continued to make notes, DeeDee checked out her surroundings again through her lashes. No mistletoe spotted, plus she wasn't sneezing or itching. "Do you have a problem with mice here? The place sat vacant for a while before you and your husband rented it. Have you hired an exterminator or put out traps or rat poison?"

"No." Laura sounded astonished by the idea, and DeeDee bit back a laugh. Given their high-dollar lifestyle, most likely the only mouse these folks had encountered was named Mickey.

She closed her notebook and sat back, keeping her attention focused on Laura. "The sheriff received a call from your husband's attorney this morning. He said you'll stand to inherit everything, correct? Seems like that would be an awful lot of money."

"What exactly are you implying, Deputy?" Laura's brown eyes narrowed. "Do you think I killed my husband for his money? Because I can assure you there was no need for me to do that."

"Why?"

"In case you haven't gotten that far in your investigation yet, my maiden name is Bickford." Laura laughed. "My father was the president of Fisher Pharmaceuticals. I have more money in my trust fund than Tucker could've ever earned in a lifetime. If anyone was going to be killed for their fortune, it would've been me, Deputy."

All righty then. Still, that didn't leave Rockwood's widow completely off the hook just yet. Jealousy could also be a powerful motivator. DeeDee tried another tactic. "I was over at the movie set earlier, and there were quite a few rumors circulating about your husband and his possible extracurricular activities with some of the other actresses. Were you aware of his affairs, Ms. Rockwood?"

The widow's expression shifted from cold and aloof to dark and stormy. "Fine. It's true. I knew Tucker had a girlfriend on the side. And she wasn't the first, either."

"Is that why you killed him?"

"Ha!" Laura snorted. "If I tried to off Tucker every time he took up with some new tramp, he would've been dead a long time ago, believe me. I was used to his dalliances. And much as I hate to disappoint you, Deputy, I didn't kill him. I have an alibi. I was at Moon-Morning Yoga yesterday when the death occurred. Like I said, it wasn't me."

That yoga class took place at three a.m. Not unusual in a town full of paranormals, with some of them only able to go out under cover of darkness. The class was popular, and even DeeDee had thought about going several times with Nia. In fact, plenty of businesses in Silver Hollow catered to their residents' odd hours.

"How do you know your husband's time of death?" DeeDee asked. The coroner's report hadn't been released yet.

"Yesterday, the other officer mentioned Tucker's body was found after sunrise. He also said my husband appeared to have been dead for two or three hours before he was found. I did the math. Why? Have you gotten that information back?"

DeeDee compressed her lips. As far as she knew, Ursula still hadn't pinpointed an exact time of death. "I'm not at liberty to disclose that, ma'am. We do know he was poisoned."

"Poisoned?" Laura's smooth tone rose slightly. "The officers yesterday said he was stabbed."

"That too."

"Oh dear." Laura wrung her hands, some of her previous hysteria apparently returning. "I hope you don't think I poisoned poor Tucker. And then stabbed him? What kind of sick person could do something like that then go skipping off to a yoga class?"

Who indeed. Unblinking, DeeDee watched Laura Rockwood dissolve into tears. She took a deep breath for patience, allowing the other woman a moment to collect herself before continuing her questioning. "Can anyone verify your location at this yoga class, ma'am?"

"Yes." Laura gave a mirthless laugh. "Unfortunately, this person also hates me. It's the woman I suspect is Tucker's new girlfriend, Gina Presti. We aren't the best of friends, for obvious reasons. We even had it out at the yoga studio that morning before class started."

"Really?" Out came the notebook again. There were lots of notes to jot down now. "Can you spell this Gina's name for me, please?"

Laura did so while DeeDee's mind raced ahead to her

next steps. If this new girlfriend was in class with Laura, then that gave them both the same alibi. To corroborate their shared alibi, she needed to call Ursula once she got back to the station and see if the ME had an updated, more accurate time of death for the victim or time the victim was moved. Maybe Gina and Laura argued while one was coming and the other going, and the exact time would rule one of them out. Or neither of them. Then again, Laura had made it sound as if her husband wasn't the most popular guy in the room. Maybe someone else killed him.

Or maybe Tucker Rockwood demanding more money from Caine Hunter had been the last straw. Then again, the protestors had complained Tucker verbally abused them. Perhaps he'd finally crossed the line with the Sunrise Group and they'd turned rabid. She finished writing down all her theories then focused on Laura again. "Any idea of your husband's itinerary on the day of his murder?"

"No. He didn't usually share how he spent his time with me." Laura sniffled and dabbed her eyes with a tissue. "I know he went to work, then maybe he fit in some time with Gina."

"Did he keep a calendar or day planner?"

"I think there's one on his laptop." Laura stood and led DeeDee down a long hall toward the back of the house and into the den where Laura had said Tucker slept many nights. A large desk sat off to one side of the room. On top was a new laptop computer, a mouse sitting on a mouse pad with the image of a bloody-fanged vampire to the left of it.

"I'll need to take the laptop into custody. Do you want me to get a warrant?" DeeDee said.

"No. Go ahead and take it. I doubt you'll find anything on it. Tucker wasn't around much to use it." Laura stood off to the side, arms crossed. "I'm surprised the officers didn't ask for it yesterday."

"They were just gathering information at that point." DeeDee got the password from Laura and typed it in. A Fitbit app appeared onscreen. "Your husband wore a tracking device?"

"Yes." Laura sighed. "Tucker was obsessed with his health, always worried about getting his precious steps in. I'm sure he had incentive to keep in shape, with all those pretty young things he liked to bed."

Yeah, no bitterness there. Not.

Exiting the app, DeeDee opened the computer's calendar instead and scanned the dates. "Looks like your husband had an appointment with the director, Caine Hunter, on Monday morning. I've also been told by several people involved with the movie that Tucker was going to quit the film if they didn't agree to pay him more money. Is that true?"

"Probably, but it was an idle threat." Laura shook her head. "Tucker did that on every movie he made. Always going on about how he was so overworked and underappreciated."

"Wouldn't the film have to fold if he dropped out? He was the headline star, right?" DeeDee asked.

"Yes, but—" Realization dawned in Laura's eyes. "You think this director killed him because he threatened to leave?"

After closing the laptop, DeeDee stood and unplugged the computer. "I'm not sure. Thank you for your time, Ms. Rockwood. I can show myself out."

CHAPTER 10

*D*eeDee left the Rockwood residence and headed directly toward Caine Hunter's address. She didn't spend much time in his chichi high-dollar community on the shores of the lake and had to double-check the coordinates in her phone to make sure she had the right estate. When she finally pulled up to the gates in front of his huge mansion, even she had to admit the views of the White Mountains and the lake from his property were amazing.

She lowered her window and pressed the call button on the security intercom system. A snooty voice with a slight English accent answered. "Deliveries are around to the side of the property."

"Oh, no. I'm not here for a delivery. This is Deputy DeeDee Clawson with the Silver Hollow Sherriff's Department. I need to ask Mr. Caine Hunter a few questions. Is he available?"

A pause. Then the gates buzzed open.

As she wound her squad car up the long driveway to the front of the home, DeeDee was struck by how truly spectacular the place was with its exterior full of brick and glass and an architectural style that reminded her of some luxurious alpine cabin. She parked her cruiser near the grand covered portico then got out, making sure that Rockwood's laptop was securely stowed beneath the seat. She straightened her uniform and walked up to the carved entry doors and knocked, using the sparkling brass knocker with a snarling wolf's head at the top.

That was odd. They were usually lions, weren't they?

Then again, Caine Hunter was a werewolf, so maybe it had to do with his pack.

Before she could contemplate it further, however, a butler answered the door. "Yes?"

Same snooty voice from the intercom. DeeDee raised her chin slightly and forced a smile. "Deputy Clawson here to meet Mr. Hunter."

"Of course." The older gentleman sniffed and gave a slight bow as he gestured for DeeDee to enter the home. The interior of the house was surprisingly cozy and warm for being so large. Lots of pine and oak and overstuffed furniture begging to be sat in. A large sweeping staircase took up one side of the foyer, and she couldn't help wondering what it would feel like to live in such a grand showpiece home.

"Deputy Clawson," Caine Hunter said, descending those same stairs now, looking as irritatingly gorgeous as always. "I hope you're here to tell me you caught Tucker's killer."

"Not yet, sir." She couldn't seem to help fidgeting under his too-perceptive amber gaze. "I have a few questions for you, if you have a moment."

"For you, Deputy?" He smiled, and her insides tingled with warmth, despite DeeDee's wishes to the contrary. "Always."

They walked into a spacious great room with a high cathedral ceiling and a huge stone fireplace with flames crackling merrily inside. Christmas lights and décor were tastefully spread around the space to add to its homey feel. He walked her over to a wraparound sofa on the far side of the room before a bank of huge windows overlooking the lake. DeeDee was about to take a seat when a familiar itch started on her arms. Soon her nose twitched too, and she did her best not to sneeze. A quick glance at the windows behind the sofa showed the culprit—a sprig of mistletoe hung over them.

Caine took a seat then patted the one beside him. "Move closer, Deputy. I promise I don't bite."

"Oh, um, maybe we could sit somewhere else." When Caine gave her a funny look, she tried to cover it by changing topics. He had the mistletoe, which had been used on Rockwood. Did he have the rat poison too? "Perhaps you could give me a tour of the rest of your house. It's really beautiful, by the way."

"I'm happy to show you around." Caine smiled again, and her knees went a bit wobbly. *Ugh.* The last thing she needed was an attraction to one of her suspects. "After we finish your questions."

"Oh, sure. Right." DeeDee tucked back a loose curl that had slipped free from the tight bun at the nape of her neck, then took a seat at the very end of the sectional sofa, as far away from the mistletoe and Caine Hunter as she could get. "I interviewed Mr. Rockwood's widow, and she confirmed that her husband was threatening to quit the movie because he wanted more money. Did you give in to his demands?"

Caine shrugged, staring down at his hands in his lap. "We negotiated."

"I see." Out came DeeDee's trusty notebook again. "I've seen Mr. Rockwood's schedule the day of his murder. Looks like he had a meeting with you that morning. Did things turn ugly?"

"Ah, I see where you're going with this, Deputy." Caine looked at her again, that darned smile of his going full-watt sexy. "You think I killed Tucker because he was threatening to quit. Hate to tell you this, but you're barking up the wrong tree. Think about it. Why would I kill the star of my own movie? Without Tucker's star power, the film could flop, and then I'd lose my entire investment."

Good point. DeeDee closed her pad and leaned back. The sofa was even cushier than it looked. It sort of wrapped around a person and encouraged them to cuddle in.

"My brother's telling the truth." Caine's sister,

Carletta, stood in the large, open doorway leading into the kitchen. "Tucker wasn't mad when he left here on Monday."

DeeDee sat forward, her wolf senses telling her there was more to this situation. Carletta was beautiful and blond. Could she and Tucker have had an affair going on as well? Maybe she knew more about the murder than she was letting on. Before she could ask, however, Caine drew her attention back to him.

"Next question, Deputy," he said. The man sprawled gracefully across his seat, one arm across the back, totally relaxed, like the king in his castle. If circumstances were different and she'd met Caine Hunter outside of work, he would've been just the kind of guy she'd go for—confident, cool, charming.

As it was, though, she had a murder to solve and far too many loose ends untied to let this guy off the hook so easily. DeeDee cleared her throat and went back through her notes. "Fine. As the producer and director of the film, Mr. Hunter, I assume you have complete and unrestricted access to everything on the movie set?"

"Yes. Why do you ask?" He cocked his head to the side and smiled. "And, please, call me Caine."

She ignored his offer. "The stake driven through Tucker Rockwood's heart came from the trailer on your set, though the prop master had no record of anyone checking one out. That means someone with a key and access had to have stolen one."

"Also not true." Carletta came into the great room and

perched on the other end of the sofa, near to her brother. "That trailer is never locked or secured properly. And I hope you're not insinuating that my brother is a thief, Deputy. He has an alibi. We were both here the night of the murder. Jarvis can attest to it."

"Jarvis?" DeeDee raised a brow.

"Our butler," Carletta said, gesturing to the older man who'd answered the door and now

reappeared with a tray of tea and freshly baked scones. They smelled scrumptious, and her stomach rumbled loudly.

Must be almost lunchtime. She frowned and fumbled with her notebook again to distract herself.

"What about all those horrid protestors?" Carletta continued. "They seem violent."

"They're on our list of suspects, ma'am." The butler handed DeeDee a dainty cup of tea, and she took it, afraid if she squeezed the handle too hard the whole thing might shatter. "Um, may I use your restroom a moment, please? I need to wash my hands."

"Of course," Caine said, fixing himself a cup of tea. "Jarvis can show you where it's at."

"Oh, no. I don't want to be a bother. Point me in the right direction, and I'm sure I can find it."

He did as she asked, exchanging a look with his sister that DeeDee didn't miss.

She headed down the hall indicated until she was out of sight then made a quick detour toward the kitchen. She needed to find out if there was any rat poison on the premises. They wouldn't keep it in the kitchen with the food, but maybe in a butler's pantry or broom closet. Those rooms could be behind one of these doors right near the kitchen in the hallway.

She quietly opened one door. Nope. Bathroom. Another door. Some kind of breakfast nook. The next door. Locked! Why would they have it locked unless they had something to hide? And if that something was a big old box of rat poison, then that could mean—

"Looking for something?" Caine asked from behind her.

Busted.

DeeDee slowly turned to face him, peeking one eye open to find him much closer to her than she expected. Close enough for her to feel the heat of him through her uniform. Close enough that if she stretched up ever so slightly, she could kiss him.

"Deputy?" he asked, his voice a tad huskier than before, a spark of heat in his eyes.

Swallowing hard, she forced herself to step back, away from temptation. Her words squeaked out far higher than intended. "I-I was looking for the bathroom and must've taken a wrong turn."

Caine watched her for a moment, giving her a slow head-to-toe appraisal that set all her nerve endings on fire. At last, he said, "It's this door over here."

Her hand still rested on the locked door, and she couldn't stop herself from asking, "What's in here?"

"Nothing you need to see." Caine stepped even closer to

her, mere inches separating them now. Her heart thumped hard in her chest, and her mouth went dry, and if she didn't get out of there right that second, she would lean in and do something she might regret later like kiss him silly.

"Right. Bathroom." DeeDee slipped out from between Caine and the wall and headed to the bathroom, feeling the weight of his stare shivering down her spine.

AN HOUR LATER, Caine watched the receding tail lights of DeeDee's squad car as she drove down his driveway and off his estate. At least the meeting tonight had proven beyond a shadow of a doubt the physical attraction between them was strong.

He'd also discovered a few more things. Things like his future wife was loyal to her friends and colleagues, diligent in her pursuit of justice, and hardworking. From what little he knew of her, DeeDee had doggedly persisted on her case, despite setbacks. This told him she would be the kind of woman who stood by her mate. She was stubborn too. And fearless. And quick on her feet. All those things only made her more attractive to him.

When he'd discovered her snooping in his hallway, as he'd suspected she would, Caine had nearly told her the truth about him, about who he was and what they would become to each other. But in the end, he'd held back, afraid of being hurt again. This time, Caine wanted to be one hundred percent certain before he opened his heart and his life again.

"She left awfully quickly," Carletta said from the doorway into the great room. "Hopefully, she's not speeding back to the sheriff's office to get a warrant for your arrest."

Caine snorted. "I don't think so. She suspects there's something going on with me, but since I didn't kill Tucker, I'm not worried. DeeDee's smart. She'll find the real murderer soon enough."

His sister smiled. "On a first-name basis now with Deputy Clawson, huh?" Carletta leaned against the huge granite-topped island in the center of the kitchen. "Maybe if you told her your true identity, dear brother, she'd knock you off the suspect list even faster."

"Or move me to the top." He exhaled and rested his forearms on the opposite side of the island.

"Oh, come on. I know you don't want to be hurt again, but you must put the needs of the pack ahead of your own, Caine. Our future depends on this marriage. You marrying DeeDee Clawson and forging a new blood treaty with her pack to protect and expand our territories must come before your own personal needs."

"I know." Caine hung his head. Still, hope flared brightly that this union might be more than just a business deal.

"So what are you waiting for?" Carletta asked. "Do you honestly think you're doing DeeDee any favors by not telling her who you really are? As a fellow woman, I can say with certainty you're not."

"No. I know that too. I just hoped…" He shrugged.

"Hoped what, Caine? Hoped for some kind of love match?" She gave him a sad little smile. "Brother, you know as well as I do how rare those are. The kinds of relationships where mates bond so deeply they share each other's emotions and finish each other's sentences. Especially with arranged unions." She moved closer and cupped his cheek. "Please stop hoping and wishing for the impossible and face your duty. It's not like you have a choice in the matter."

He nodded, and Carletta kissed his cheek before wandering away back into the great room. Caine stayed in the kitchen, alone, pondering his situation. Once DeeDee found out who he was, it would change everything between them. Cloud all their interactions. There'd be no more sizzling chemistry, no more teasing, no more stolen moments in secret rooms.

And he just wasn't ready to give all that up yet. Not with her. It was too sweet. He wanted to savor their interactions a bit longer before it all came to a sudden, irreversible end. And despite what his sister had said, Caine refused to give up hope.

Hope that perhaps, by some miracle, DeeDee might come to love him for who he was and not because she had an obligation to her pack.

CHAPTER 11

*D*eeDee thought about heading back to headquarters and running a background check on Caine Hunter, but given the sparks between them inside his house, maybe she should wait on that. Then there was the fact the yoga studio was on the way and she needed to stop there to corroborate Laura Rockwood's alibi.

So, instead, she pulled over to the curb, put the cruiser in park, and called Dex.

"Silver Hollow Sheriff's Department. This is Detective Nolan speaking."

"Hey, buddy. It's DeeDee."

"Oh, hey. How's it going? I haven't seen you around all day."

"I know." She fiddled with the buttons on the front of her coat. "I've been busy investigating the Rockwood murder." *And flirting with my prime suspect.* DeeDee squeezed her eyes shut and shook off the lingering warmth in her blood each time she remembered the heat in Caine's amber eyes. "Listen, I need you to do me a favor, if you have the time."

"Sure thing. What do you need?"

"Can you run a background check for me?" She rattled off Caine Hunter's name and demographics. "Thanks. What's going on there today?"

"Ugh, be glad you're not here."

"Why?"

"Stan came back from another trip to the morgue," Dex said, his tone flat. "And he's acting all weird again."

"Weird how?"

"Like he's not his usual gung-ho, let's-catch-all-the-paranormals self." Dex sighed. "Do you think Ursula did something to him?"

"Is it an improvement?" DeeDee asked.

Dex chuckled. "Yeah, it is."

"Then who cares if she did something to him?"

"Good point. I'll get this background check started as soon as we hang up. Where are you headed to next?"

"I talked to Rockwood's widow again earlier and got her alibi. She says she was taking the Moon-Morning Yoga class at the time of Tucker's death. So I'm headed over there to check it out."

"Cool. You want to meet me later at the place where that napkin was from? The Coffee Connection?" Dex asked. "I can give you the background check results and get some much-needed caffeine at the same time. Hang on." The tapping sounds of fingers on a keyboard filled the phone line, then Dex came back on the line. "Looks like the place is about halfway between the yoga studio and headquarters. Maybe someone there saw Tucker and can give us a new lead."

"Sounds good, buddy." DeeDee smiled. "See you in an hour?"

"Perfect. See you then."

They ended the call, and DeeDee signaled before pulling out into traffic again.

About half an hour later, she was parked in front of a small strip mall where the yoga studio was located. Inside, the air was filled with soothing New Age music and the tinkle of chimes. A small reception desk sat to one side of the entrance, and a skinny girl in black leggings and a pink sports bra sat filing her nails. Her nose ring glittered beneath the overhead lights. The girl's eyes widened slightly as DeeDee stepped up to the counter.

"Can I help you?" she asked, staring at the gun holstered at DeeDee's waist.

"Uh, hi. Yeah. I've got some questions about your Moon-Morning yoga classes."

"Great." The girl finally managed to look DeeDee in the eye. "Would you like to sign up? We have new classes starting all the time and offer a range of difficulty levels from beginner to advanced."

"Oh, thanks. But no. I'm not here for myself. Did you have a class yesterday morning?"

"Sure," the girl said. "We have them every morning. They're very popular around here, especially with all those movie people in town."

"May I see the roster, please?" This time DeeDee showed her badge. "Official law enforcement business."

"Um, sure." The girl pulled out a clipboard from the drawer beside her and passed it over the counter.

DeeDee flipped through the pages, and sure enough, she found both Laura Rockwood and Gina Presti's names on the list. Pointing to them, DeeDee asked, "Can you verify both these people were in the class yesterday morning?"

"Those two? Oh yeah. Hard to forget when they got into a fight near the end of class. I'm bummed because I never got to see what was happening before they broke it up. I miss out on all the good stuff because I'm stuck behind this desk all the time. Not to mention I never got a piece of the pie."

"Pie?" DeeDee asked.

"I saw Gina coming into class carrying some sort of pie in a bag. Must have been juicy too because she didn't want to spill it." The girl mimed carrying a tray in front of her, palms spread out flat. "Probably blueberry."

Why would Gina bring a pie to yoga? DeeDee's suspicious mind thought about poison, but Tucker was already dead at that point. Maybe the yoga class worked up an appetite and people brought snacks.

"What time would you say that fight took place?"

DeeDee pulled out her notepad again to jot down the answer.

"Easy," the girl said. "Those classes run from three thirty to four thirty each morning like clockwork, and those two got into it right before the end of class, so I'd say maybe four fifteen."

"Great. Thank you."

DeeDee walked out of the yoga studio to find Dex parked next to her cruiser. "Hey, I was just on my way over to the coffee shop."

"I'm a little early. Had to get out of the office for a while." Dex held up a cup of joe and another for her. She took it gratefully. "I drove by The Coffee Connection," he said. "Saw you weren't there yet, so I decided to head on over here. After grabbing us energy to go, of course."

"Thanks. Did you get the results of my background check?"

"I did. I also got some new information from the reports Stan brought back from Ursula about the victim's body."

"Yeah." She took a long swig of her coffee. "What'd she find?"

"Splinters."

"Splinters?"

"Yeah, lots of them, lodged in the victim's body. Ursula thinks they might've become embedded when Rockwood was moved. Did you see any wooden carts or floors or anything that might've caused them when you were at the movie set earlier?"

"No." DeeDee frowned. "Then again, I wasn't really looking. You want to head back over there with me now and we can check it out together? I'll bring you back here after we're done to get your car."

"Sure." Dex climbed into the passenger seat of the cruiser while DeeDee got behind the wheel and started the engine. "I can give you the rundown on Caine Hunter's background check on the way over."

"Perfect." DeeDee pulled out of the lot and headed back toward the Crenshaw mansion. "So what did you find? Is it awful?"

"No." Dex squinted out the window into the sunshine. "There was just something a bit off about it. Not anything the average person would notice, but with my FBI training, I always look a little deeper. I have this sinking feeling Caine Hunter isn't who he says he is."

His observations only made her own suspicions rise higher. She'd felt that the guy was holding something back when she'd interviewed him earlier, and this only confirmed it. Still, she didn't want to go inventing some trouble where none existed either. It wasn't unusual for werewolf pack names to get changed over time, or for members to adopt assumed names because they didn't want favors because of their pack association. So, on the positive side, maybe Caine Hunter wanted to earn his movie producer credits on his own.

That was something DeeDee could respect.

They pulled up to the movie set and got out. The Sunrise Group was still at it, as were the guards who let her and Dex inside. She led him over to the props trailer, and together they searched the cluttered interior once more. It didn't take long to find something.

"Over here," DeeDee called to Dex, who was searching through crap on the other end of the trailer. He walked over, and she pointed to what she'd found. "A wooden dolly. It's got wheels too, for easy transport. Looks like the perfect size to move a body, and the top is all rough and splintery."

The Fae prop master still lurked around the perimeter, and DeeDee gestured toward them. "Hey, remember me? I was here this morning. Listen, we need to know how many of these wooden dollies you have lying around."

"That's the only one," the prop master said.

"Look at this one wheel too," Dex said, crouching beside the thing. "There's mud caked on it. The size looks about right for those tracks we found near Rockwood's body too."

"Hey, Sam," Caine Hunter said, charging up the ramp and into the shadowed interior of the trailer. He blinked several times as his vision adjusted from the brightness outside, then frowned down at DeeDee. "What are you doing here, Deputy?"

She squared her shoulders against the unwanted attraction for him flooding her system. "I'm trying to figure out who killed Tucker Rockwood. How about you?"

Caine gave her a flat stare. "I'm trying to make a movie. In case you haven't noticed, your investigation has disrupted my entire shooting schedule. Not to mention the workarounds I haven't even had a chance to deal with yet because Tucker's gone."

"Oh, I'm sorry. Did his death inconvenience you?" DeeDee crossed her arms, her booted toe tapping against the metal floor of the trailer. Some part of her knew her attraction for this man was the source of her irritation, but that didn't stop her from letting him have it. "How thoughtless of the guy to go and get himself murdered."

Dex coughed to cover an inappropriate snort and joined the prop master on the other side of the trailer.

"That's not what I meant, and you know it."

"No, I don't know, Mr. Hunter. In fact, I don't know much about you at all. Typical Hollywood type, nothing but smoke and mirrors."

"I'm sorry." Caine's gaze narrowed. "Do you have some kind of problem with me?"

"Yeah, as a matter of fact, I do." DeeDee stepped closer to him, poking her index finger into the middle of his muscled chest. "How do I know you didn't run in here to tamper with evidence?"

"Excuse me?" Caine scowled and moved closer still to her, so close his front now brushed hers and sent all sorts of wicked zings of awareness through her. "What evidence?"

"Uh, that would be this cart," Dex said, interceding at last.

Shaken, DeeDee stepped back from Caine, shocked at how close she'd come to tackling him to the floor of the trailer and kissing him. Cheeks pulsating with heat, she kept her gaze lowered as Dex continued.

"We think it might have been used by Rockwood's killer to transport the body to its final resting place."

Caine shook his head then looked to the prop master. "Who used this cart last night, Sam?"

"I don't know, sir. My day ended at eight on Monday, and I locked up and left shortly afterward." The Fae shrugged. "When I came in Tuesday morning, it was back here again."

"Can you tell us who has access to this trailer besides the prop master?" Dex asked Caine. DeeDee still stood off to the side, not trusting herself to speak quite yet. There was something about this guy that made her throw caution to the wind and become distracted. For a gal like her, distraction was dangerous. People died when DeeDee wasn't careful.

Cursing, Caine tromped back down the ramp and lifted a large rock on the ground near the corner of the trailer. Beneath it was a set of keys. "I know this looks bad, but you have to understand that making a movie involves creativity. I don't like to limit my crew. Sometimes the most brilliant ideas strike in the middle of the night. So we always keep a set of keys available for anyone to use to get the props they need."

Taking her opportunity for escape, DeeDee ran back to her car and grabbed the crime scene tape then returned to cordon off the dolly. "No one touches this until our crime scene techs have processed it. It's too big to fit in the cruiser, so we'll have to leave it here for now until we can get the crew in. Understand?"

Caine nodded, not meeting DeeDee's gaze.

"Come on. Let's go," she said at last, tugging on Dex's arm as she passed. "I'll radio in for the CSI crew on our way back to headquarters."

The drive back into Silver Hollow proper was oddly quiet. She couldn't help remembering Caine's genuine confusion when she'd asked him about the dolly. Her instincts told her he wasn't the killer, but she still had to do her due diligence. To slack off now could mean that the real murderer would go free, which was unacceptable.

Then there was this niggling sense of connection blossoming out of nowhere inside her. Worse, the feeling intensified whenever Caine was around. It was as if she could sense his thoughts and feelings. Which was ridiculous. Sure, she'd heard about such things happening with true-soul-mate-bonded werewolves, but that couldn't be what was happening.

First, she was pledged to marry another man. Second, Caine was a suspect in her murder investigation. And third... Well, she couldn't think of a third reason right now, but the first two were bad enough.

Dex practically stared a hole in the side of her head until DeeDee finally stopped for a red light and faced him. "What?"

"Nothing." He held his hands up in surrender at her snippy tone. "I just noticed how you and Hunter got into it back there and wondered if there was something I should know."

She frowned. "Like what?"

"I don't know. Like maybe you two were dating or something. I thought I sensed something there."

The light turned green, and DeeDee accelerated again. "Well, you sensed wrong. There's nothing between Caine Hunter and me, okay? Just forget it."

"Fine. Consider it forgotten." Dex stared out the window beside him again. "That's good. I mean, he could be the killer. But if he's not, then if maybe someday something did start with you and him, things could proceed as normal."

"Proceed as normal?" DeeDee scrunched her nose as they turned the corner and rounded the main green at the center of Silver Hollow's downtown to head back toward the strip mall and Dex's car. "That's about as unromantic a statement as I think I've ever heard, Dexter Nolan." She snorted. "And here I thought you'd gone all mushy since you fell for Issy Quinn."

"I will never be mushy." He gave her a look. "And maybe what I said didn't come out right, but I stand behind the sentiment. You're a good person, DeeDee, and a wonderful cop. You deserve to be happy." He grinned. "And mushy or not, I've never gotten any complaints from Issy."

Laughing, DeeDee pulled into the strip mall parking lot. "It's nice to see you two so happy."

"Yeah, life's pretty great with the right person." His

expression went all goofy with love. DeeDee rolled her eyes. "Hey, don't knock it until you try it, Deputy."

"Right. Sure. Now get out of my cruiser before you start oozing hearts and rainbows." Dex chuckled and climbed out. "I'll see you back at the station."

"Yep." He waved then climbed into his own car and started the engine.

Still, DeeDee couldn't shake the frustration beneath her surface. So much so she lowered the passenger-side window and flagged down Dex. "Hey, you up for another cup of joe?"

"Lead the way," he said.

CHAPTER 12

"So you never told me what you found out at the yoga studio," Dex said as they met up at the entrance to The Coffee Connection. They walked inside and found the place surprisingly busy for a midweek midafternoon. The interior had a nice modern, industrial feel, with lots of exposed brick, overhead steel pipes, and earthy colors. A large glass display case near the register was filled with yummy homemade bagels and treats, and DeeDee's stomach rumbled anew. After all, she'd only had one scone at Caine's place, and that had been a few hours ago. She was due for another snack, right?

"Well, she was there, all right, according to the receptionist, anyway. Along with the woman she thinks her husband was having an affair with, Gina Presti."

Dex cringed. "How'd that go down?"

"Not well." DeeDee snorted. "They got into a fight near the end of the class. That's how the receptionist remembered them being there." She stepped up to the counter and ordered a large cappuccino and a cinnamon crunch bagel with cream cheese. Dex ordered the same.

"Apparently, the receptionist wasn't happy about not getting to see the catfight," DeeDee continued as she paid her bill then moved down to the end of the counter to wait for her order. Dex followed behind her. "So yeah. Not having a clear time of death for the victim doesn't help, since we can't clear either woman yet. Laura Rockwood had a point, though. What kind of sicko would poison her husband then go to a yoga class afterward?"

"Her?" Dex asked.

"Not sure," DeeDee said. "Maybe."

"Clawson!" the man behind the counter called, and DeeDee stepped up to the counter to grab her order. The guy, decked out in a Santa hat, was the owner of the place.

"Thanks." DeeDee grabbed her coffee and bagel then narrowed her gaze on the man. "Hey. As owner of The Coffee Connection, you must spend a lot of time here."

"All of it, it seems like." He smiled. "Why?"

"We're investigating the murder of Tucker Rockwood. Did you ever see him in here?"

He passed Dex his order then leaned his hip against the counter. "Yeah, Tucker came in a lot. He was here on Monday, in fact, with some hot young blonde. They looked pretty friendly too, if you know what I mean."

Dex gave DeeDee a look.

"Did anything out of the ordinary happen while they were here?" she asked.

"Hmm." The owner frowned. "Let me think. You know, now that you mention it, he did seem to get into it with a couple of those protestors. They come in here a lot too." He nodded toward a group of them in one corner of the shop. "Weird bunch. Almost like a cult."

DeeDee scrunched her nose. Yeah, they were troublesome and rude, but that didn't make them a cult. "What do you mean?"

"Look at their hair," the shop owner said. "Same cut on all of them, men and women. Sort of long and scruffy. And those patches on their jackets—blue mountains with an orange-and-yellow sun rising above them. I know they call themselves the Sunrise Group, but I swear there's more going on there than just simple protest marches."

"Huh." DeeDee grabbed her stuff and turned to Dex. "Let's eat outside in the car, eh?"

"Uh, sure." They went out, and she got into the cruiser while Dex started his old Buick to let the engine run while they talked. He then climbed into her passenger seat. "So what do you think about what the owner said? Think those protestors had something to do with Rockwood's death?"

DeeDee spread thick cream cheese on her bagel with the cheap plastic knife the shop had put in her bag, then took a bite, savoring the sweet crunch of the cinnamon chips and the creamy goodness of the cheese. She took a swig of coffee to wash it all down before answering. "I think we need to add them to the list of suspects. Can't rule out anybody yet."

"Not even Caine Hunter?"

"Especially Caine Hunter," she said around another bite of bagel. Her stomach did that strange little flip it always did whenever his name came up, but she shook it off and focused on her case. "The only thing we can verify at this point is that Hunter met with Tucker on the day of his murder. They argued about money, which is always a dangerous subject."

"True." Dex finished his bagel in three bites then shoved his trash back in his bag. "But I really can't see him offing the guy. I mean, Tucker Rockwood's star power was carrying that whole movie. Why would Hunter tank his investment in the movie by taking out the lead actor?"

"Yeah, that's what I thought too." DeeDee devoured her last bite of food, hating to admit Caine had made the same good point when she'd talked to him earlier, but unable to deny it either. "So I guess we're left with the wife and protestors. Maybe the girlfriend too. The shop owner said Tucker was in there with her the day he died. Perhaps she wanted Tucker to leave his wife and got mad when he refused. Did I tell you the widow's worth way more than Rockwood could ever hope to be?" She filled Dex in about Laura being the daughter of a pharmaceutical tycoon. "With that kind of money in play, it would be hard for Tucker to leave."

"And you said she knew about Tucker cheating too and didn't seem to care much." Dex shook his head. "That kind of freedom would be hard for certain men to walk away from."

"Yeah." DeeDee took her trash and Dex's and tossed it in the garbage bin outside the entrance to The Coffee Connection then returned to the car. "So I guess I'll add the girlfriend to my list of people to interview."

"We need to nail down the exact location where the murder took place too. It's going to be difficult to confirm alibis if we can't place the killer with the body at a specific time."

"I wish that movie set had surveillance cameras." DeeDee leaned down and checked to make sure Tucker Rockwood's laptop was still securely under her seat. "At least I got the victim's computer while I talked to the grieving wife. Pulled up his calendar and saw he had a meeting scheduled that night. No name or place listed, of course."

"Figures." Dex snorted.

"I know, right?" DeeDee frowned. "Wait a minute. He had a FitBit."

"What?"

"A FitBit. You know, those exercise tracking bracelets. He was wearing it the night he was killed. I'm sure it's back at the station, in the evidence room along with the rest of his personal effects," DeeDee said, her adrenaline building. "When I first looked at Rockwood's laptop, the app with his data was pulled up. I read a newspaper article not long ago involving a tracker like this. It's a long shot, but there might be a way we can figure out exactly when Tucker's body was moved to the final location."

CAINE STOPPED at a red light on his way back from the Moon-Morning Yoga Studio. He'd gone there after DeeDee had mentioned the place when she'd questioned him earlier. Caine had meant what he'd said in that props trailer. He wanted to catch Tucker Rockwood's killer as much, if not more, than law enforcement. After all, he had much more at stake. Not just money, but his innocence.

He glanced over and saw DeeDee's squad car parked in front of a new little coffee shop called The Coffee Connection. He'd not been to the place himself yet, but a couple members of his crew frequented the shop. Tucker had gone there too a few times, if he wasn't mistaken.

As Caine watched, the passenger door of DeeDee's car opened, and the detective who'd been with her back at his film set got out then got into a vintage black Buick parked beside the cruiser.

A horn honked behind him, jolting Caine's attention back to the road ahead. That was what he got for taking the Mercedes out himself this afternoon instead of calling for his driver. Smiling, he waved to the irate driver behind him then sped off through the green light. In his rearview mirror, he saw both the detective and DeeDee pull out of the parking lot and head toward downtown Silver Hollow.

Man, she was so dedicated to her job. Caine was dedicated too, to his art and his pack, but he wasn't sure if it was to the same degree as DeeDee. He admired her tenacity and the fact she wasn't just another fluffy airhead, like the women who usually flocked his way in Hollywood. Or like that receptionist back at the yoga place. She'd all but drooled over him as she'd answered his questions. When he was younger, he would've been all over her like white on rice. Now, though, he wanted more.

He wanted DeeDee.

The thought both alarmed and amazed him. Amazed him because, honestly, when his father had first made the deal with DeeDee's dad, Caine hadn't been happy.

Yes, he understood it was his responsibility and his duty to serve the pack. Someday he'd take over for his father and be alpha, and with that position came certain burdens—like ensuring the pack would have sufficient lands to roam and maintaining cordial relationships with their neighbors. He'd understood this marriage contract was strictly political, strictly a way to secure his pack and their lands for the next generation, so he'd not expected much to come from his marriage to DeeDee. Especially given most women of his acquaintance only seemed interested in his money, fame, and status. His old flame, Brenda, had certainly fit that mold.

But DeeDee was different. And yes, maybe it was stupid for him to be all the way out here in the middle of nowhere to film a movie that had been iffy at best, even before Tucker's death. He was hemorrhaging money by the day, and the script was a mess, and now, with his leading star gone, he'd have to be here even longer to reshoot the earlier scenes so they could somehow salvage what was left of this wreck of a film and try to recoup some of the lost funds.

Still, Caine couldn't bring himself to regret his choice to come to Silver Hollow. He'd done it because of DeeDee. He'd wanted a chance to romance her, to get to know her without their relationship being clouded by the fact of their forced marriage.

Too bad this murder investigation had now ruined those plans too.

He'd sensed DeeDee liked him too. In a way that went beyond normal instincts, beyond anything he'd ever known. It almost felt like telepathy, as though he knew what she would say or do before she did. Like the kind of bond soul-mated wolves developed.

He sighed and turned down the street toward the Crenshaw mansion and his movie set. Maybe Carletta was right. Maybe he should've told DeeDee who he was from the start. Maybe if he had, he could've avoided all this mess happening now with Tucker's death and her putting him at the top of her suspect list for the murder.

Caine had a feeling once she found out that he'd lied to her about his identity, he'd be at the top of another of her lists too. The course of love never did run smoothly, but he feared he'd damaged his one chance at true love beyond any hope of recovery.

CHAPTER 13

*B*ack at headquarters, DeeDee bypassed her desk and headed straight for the evidence room. After collecting the box of Tucker's personal things, she brought it to Owen's office and set it on his desk. Inside was the black FitBit bracelet, cataloged and tagged as coming from the victim's left wrist.

"What's going on?" Owen asked, returning to the room with a can of soda in his hand. He cracked open the top and took a swig. "Find out anything interesting today?"

She brought him up to date on her interviews then showed him the tracking device. "I told Dex I think we might be able to use this to discover when the victim's body was moved."

"Huh." He shook his head then took a seat. "Never heard of anything like that before."

"Yep." She closed the evidence box then carried it

back to her own desk in the corner. "I read an article in the paper a few months back where another police department used the steps recorded on a FitBit to prove a suspect couldn't have been where he'd said he was because of the amount of steps recorded on the device."

"Dang, Deputy." Owen chuckled. "You're becoming a regular Bill Gates."

DeeDee laughed. "Hardly. I'm not an expert on these things by any means, but I'm hoping if the victim was still wearing it at the time his body was moved, it recorded something that might allow us to determine the time."

Dex walked in and plopped down in his chair then fired up his computer. "Want me to Google that thing to see how it works?"

"Sure." DeeDee took off her coat then joined Dex, leaning her hip against the side of his chair. He frowned at the screen, squinting. "Says here they only record steps when the wearer is moving forward or up and down, like walking, so it doesn't mistakenly record when you're doing other stuff, like riding in a car."

"Well, that won't help us much then." She sighed. "Let's say Tucker died at one in the morning. He certainly wouldn't have been walking to the place where we found his body at two."

Stan stumbled in, looking more like a zombie than a human. His skin was deathly pale, and dark circles shadowed his eyes. DeeDee and the guys exchanged a look as poor Stan fumbled to his desk against the wall and slumped into his seat.

"Hey there, Agent Judge," Owen said, his expression concerned. "We were just talking about the Tucker Rockwood case. What are your thoughts on the matter?"

"Whatever you guys think is fine," Stan mumbled then looked away. DeeDee spotted two puncture marks on the side of Stan's neck, and her eyes widened. It looked as if Mr. FBPI had been doing more than investigating when he'd met with Ursula. Stan tilted his head and slowly glanced back at Owen, listless. "Do you need me to check on anything at the morgue?"

Owen frowned. "No. You just came from there. I think we're good for now. Are you sure you're okay? You don't seem to be your usual gung-ho self on this investigation."

"Whatever." Stan swiveled his chair away from them to stare at the wall.

DeeDee focused her attention back on the case at hand. "Right. So this FitBit."

"Hard to believe you could figure out so much from a bracelet," Owen said.

"Not from the bracelet." DeeDee smiled. Owen was a great sheriff but not the most tech-savvy guy in the world. "From the wireless recorder inside. It sends the data to the app connected to it." She waved him over to Dex's desk then popped out the little black gadget to show him. "See? This is connected to an app that stores the data. The same app that was open on Rockwood's computer when I first logged on in his den." She moved back to her own desk and fired up Tucker's laptop. "Let me pull that app up again."

Dex and Owen moved in on either side of her. Stan was still staring at the wall.

"Here." She tapped a button, and up popped Tucker's daily log and timeline of his steps. DeeDee pointed to a graph on the screen. "Look how his activity level dropped off sharply after one in the morning. Then there was nothing, just like Ursula said."

At the mention of the vampire coroner, Stan turned to face them abruptly, his eyes glazed. "Somebody say Ursula? Want me to go see her again?"

"I think we got it, Stan," Dex said. "Go back to work."

"Work," Stan mumbled, slowly turning back around to face the wall again.

"He's a bit under the weather," Dex said, giving DeeDee some serious side-eye.

"Got that right." She snorted as she scrolled down the screen. "The recorder shows his body started moving again around three fifty a.m."

"Yeah, right." Owen scoffed. "How does a dead guy move his arms up and down?"

"Dex and I found a dolly at the movie set we think was used to transport the body from the initial location where Rockwood was killed to the place where we found the body later. I dispatched a crime scene crew out there to process it." She looked up at them. "If Tucker's hand slipped off the dolly as he was being moved, that would account for the up and down motion needed to record these steps."

"It would also account for his left hand being mangled when we found him," Dex said.

"Yep." DeeDee moved farther down the screen. "The recording stops again at four seventeen a.m. Nothing after that."

"Looks like we've got our time for the body drop." Dex straightened.

"So if his killer used this dolly to move the body and the stake wasn't embedded deeply in the victim's chest, it could very well have been a female who murdered him. You still think the wife did it?" Owen asked.

"No, not given her alibi. Couldn't have been the girl-friend either." DeeDee pulled out her notebook and showed them her notes. "They were both in yoga class during that time. I verified it with the studio."

"Great." Dex scrubbed a hand over his face. "Who else does that leave us with then?"

DeeDee opened the evidence box again and searched inside, hoping for another clue. The swatch of blue fabric she collected that day from the fence line caught her eye.

"What about this?" She pulled out the small evidence bag. "This color looks an awful lot like the emblem those protestors wear. Maybe one of them snuck inside the gates."

"Could be," Dex said.

"Now that I think about it, the day I interviewed Levi Harding, he wasn't wearing his black jacket like the rest of the Sunrise Group. I remember at the time thinking it was strange because it was so cold out." She flipped back through the pages of her notebook. "I even jotted something down here about it. Maybe he wasn't wearing his jacket because he'd ripped the sleeve while sneaking inside to murder Tucker."

wenty minutes later, DeeDee sped back to the Crenshaw mansion. As she pulled into the driveway, she saw only a few protestors milling about in front of the gates. It was after five now, and the temperatures had dropped, putting the wind chills well below zero, so that could explain it.

She got out of her cruiser and trudged up to the gates, her hood up and her hands encased in thick gloves, preventing her from taking notes. She pulled one woman aside. "Where is everyone?"

"We took shifts," the woman said. "Because of the extreme cold."

"Right." DeeDee frowned. "Is Levi Harding back at the hotel?"

"Yep. He's not due for a shift again until after midnight."

"Great. Thanks." DeeDee rushed back to her car and

peeled out of the driveway. The last thing she wanted was Levi Harding skipping town. She pulled off her gloves and cranked the heater in the squad car then used the Bluetooth to call the Route Nine Motel's manager—who was paranormal and one of her best informants—and got Levi's room number. When she pulled into the lot a short time later, she went directly to Harding's room instead of the office. He answered on her second knock.

"What are you doing here?" Levi frowned. He was dressed in boxers and a T-shirt, clearly not expecting company.

"I need to ask you a few more questions, Mr. Harding." DeeDee glanced past him and into the messy motel room. She wasn't itching or sneezing, so there was no mistletoe present, but that didn't mean he wasn't hiding rat poison in there somewhere.

He sighed and stepped aside, allowing her to enter. "Fine. What else do you need to know?"

"Where were you between three forty and four seventeen on Tuesday night when Tucker Rockwood was murdered?" DeeDee made a check around the room for rat poison or pesticide as she questioned him.

"Here. Asleep, just like I told you before." Harding's gaze darted sideways as he answered, a clear indication he was lying. Her instincts went on high alert.

She noticed his black jacket tossed on a chair in the corner of the room and made her way over to it. Yep, the sleeve was torn right where the patch was sewn, a hunk of it torn out. DeeDee held the damaged coat up for him to see. "We found evidence at the crime scene matching the missing fabric from this jacket, Mr. Harding. I'm betting if we tested the cloth and fibers, it would be a perfect match to your jacket. Why don't you save us the time and trouble and just confess to what you've done? Make it easy on yourself, Mr. Harding."

Levi's big frame seemed to crumple, and he sank down on the edge of his bed. "All right. Fine. I did sneak onto the film set that night but not to kill Tucker Rockwood. I'm dating one of the actresses in the movie, but we have to keep it a secret."

DeeDee removed her gloves and got out her trusty notebook again. "Why do you have to keep this affair a secret?"

"I'm the head of the Sunrise Group. How would it look if someone found out I'm fooling around with one of the very people we're protesting against?" He looked up at her, his expression imploring. "Please don't tell anyone. It would ruin everything."

"I'll need this actress's name." DeeDee frowned. "Give it to me, and I'll see what I can do."

His whole explanation sounded sketchy at best, but she scribbled down the name Levi gave her anyway then shoved her pad back in her pocket. "I'll need to question your girlfriend to have her corroborate your story."

"It's gonna be hard for you to find the real killer."

"Why's that, Mr. Harding?" DeeDee asked as she pulled on her gloves again.

"That set's teeming with people at night. That's why I

had to skulk around, to stay hidden and not have people notice me. Most of the folks hang out near the main mansion house."

"What about near where the body was found? Do people hang out around there too?"

"No, not around down by the swamp so much," Harding said. "Anyway, I saw things people did around the set when they thought no one was looking."

"Things like what?" DeeDee raised a brow.

"Take Tucker Rockwood. I saw him hanging out with a certain blonde Monday night—inside the mansion's old carriage house—and they weren't exactly running lines, if you know what I mean."

DeeDee sighed. "We already know Rockwood was cheating on his wife with one of the actresses. Gina Presti."

"Yeah? Well then, I guess good old Tucker did pretty good then, because the blonde I saw him with wasn't Gina."

"How do you know?"

"Because I saw her that night too," Levi said. "Right after I spotted Rockwood in the carriage house. Gina walked in front of me, heading toward the trailers."

If that was true, then they had yet another woman to find, and DeeDee had no time to waste. She headed for the door. "Thanks for your time, Mr. Harding. I'll show myself out."

She'd no sooner made it back to the sidewalk, however, than she nearly collided with the man who'd been foremost in her thoughts lately, whether she wanted him there or not.

Caine Hunter.

"Why are you here?" she asked, her tone as brisk as the freezing air. "This is an active law enforcement investigation. You have no place here. Unless you're trying to cover up evidence."

"I'm not trying to cover up anything," Caine said, his irritation levels matching her own, if his expression was any indication. "How many times must I tell you I had absolutely nothing to gain from Tucker's death, DeeDee?"

That was the first time she'd heard him use her name. A harsh gust of wind whistled past them, and they huddled nearer to the brick wall of the hotel, mere inches apart. Even through her heavy coat and gloves, Caine's heat penetrated through her, warming her from the inside out. DeeDee had the crazy urge to snuggle closer to him and...

No. That was silly. That was wrong. That was *impossible*.

That made absolutely no difference to her traitorous desires.

She scowled from inside her hood, her frustration levels rising in more ways than one. "Listen, Mr. Hunter. I've still not narrowed my search down to one prime suspect, which means you are still very much on my list."

"Caine," he said, his broad shoulders hunched beneath his thick cashmere coat. A brown knit skullcap was pulled down over his ears, and he still looked ridiculously handsome, darn it.

"Excuse me?" DeeDee couldn't stop herself from inching closer to his body heat. It was basically survival in these brutal elements. At least that was the excuse she was going with, anyway. Come to think of it, maybe finding out Caine Hunter was the killer wouldn't be so bad after all. Perhaps that would cure this unwelcome, unruly, untamable attraction she had for him.

"After all that's happened, I think you can call me by my first name, don't you?"

Well, crap.

If she called him by his first name, then manners demanded she allow him to keep using hers too. "Fine. Caine. Why don't you tell me why you're here tonight? Seems odd you'd show up right after me to this motel."

He didn't answer right away, his amber gaze flicking her lips. "It's a free country, DeeDee."

More stupid tingles flared inside her when her name rolled off his lips again, sweet and slow, like pure honey. Her knees quaked from the sheer force. *No, no, no.* This wasn't happening. She had a case to solve, a murder to investigate. DeeDee squeezed her eyes shut and forced her thoughts back to the task at hand. Levi Harding had mentioned Tucker messing around with another blonde. Could it have been Caine's sister, Carletta? If she'd somehow gotten messed up in this, that would explain why Caine was hanging around down here on the wrong side of Silver Hollow. She started to ask him, only to find him so close now she could see the tiny flecks of green in his gorgeous amber eyes.

Time to go.

"I need to get out of here," DeeDee said, rushing to her squad car. "I suggest you do the same, Mr. Hunter, before I start to think there's more reason for your presence than just tampering with evidence."

She started her engine and took off before Caine could stop her.

CHAPTER 15

*W*ell past her usual quitting time, DeeDee headed home. She was tired. Exhausted. She slogged inside her house and checked her answering machine as she tugged off her thick outerwear.

Still no message from her dad. Her shoulders slumped farther.

One clue. That was all she wanted. Just one small clue as to the identity of the man she was supposed to marry. As if the uncertainty weren't bad enough, now she was developing all these crazy feelings for the last man she should ever want—Caine Hunter.

She changed into her comfy PJ's, washed her face, then made herself soup for dinner before settling back into her favorite chair by the fire and getting online to research mistletoe. She'd had no luck finding any of the other things Ursula thought might have contributed to Tucker Rockwood's poisoning, like the rat poison or the fertilizer, so she decided to focus on her least favorite plant instead.

Besides, the killer could've already gotten rid of the other things, but with it being the holiday season, they'd leave the mistletoe around, in plain sight, and no one would think twice. Raine Quinn had mentioned a species that might not affect DeeDee's allergies as much. Was there also a species that was more potent? One that would make a lethal poison?

Who knew there were so many varieties? And who knew that mistletoe was a parasitic plant that grew on other trees? And who knew there was one variety whose leaves were a little slimmer that was more toxic than the others? DeeDee committed the picture of that variety to memory. Had she seen it somewhere during the investigation? She wasn't sure.

Once she'd done her research, she logged into the sheriff's department portal and ran her own background checks on both Caine and his sister, Carletta. Not that she didn't trust what Dex had told her, but she wanted to make sure all her bases were covered. Old habits died hard.

Unfortunately, he'd been right. Neither check showed anything significant, and both looked odd. There was something off about each of them, and she had to wonder once more exactly what Caine Hunter was hiding. Perhaps she'd been right to be suspicious about his sister and he was covering for her.

Tomorrow, she planned to go back to the movie set to

talk to the actress Levi Harding said he was involved with to verify her story. She also needed to talk to Gina Presti too. The fact Levi had mentioned seeing her that night, along with Laura Rockwood fighting with her at the yoga studio during the time that Tucker's body was moved, seemed more than enough to eliminate her as a suspect, but perhaps Gina had seen something that might help lead DeeDee to the real killer.

The more complicated this case became, the more her old fears and anxieties rose. Now, more than ever, she needed to stay vigilant, needed to cover all her bases, needed to not screw up anything even one bit, or risk the whole case falling apart before her very eyes.

Just like what had happened to poor Paige...

DeeDee finished typing up her report on the interview with Levi Harding then clicked Enter to put it into the system so Owen could see it first thing in the morning.

Her computer dinged, signaling a new incoming message, and kept her from being sucked under by the riptide of painful memories now swamping her mind. DeeDee shook them off and clicked the Messenger icon at the bottom of her screen, exhaled, and smiled.

Threads99 to the rescue again.

She closed the law enforcement portal and switched over to the embroidery chat room. As she typed, DeeDee reached down and grabbed her appaloosa work in progress and took another picture to send to Threads.

"Looking good," her online friend messaged back.

"Hey, what's the best way to stitch stamens on an orchid?"

Smile widening, DeeDee typed in her response. If only real life could be as simple as this online reality, where embroidery and making cross-stitch and French knots were all she had to worry about.

CHAPTER 16

The next morning, DeeDee walked into the office to find Owen dressed in another of his loud Hawaiian shirts and a pair of board shorts. The shirt she expected. The shorts? Not so much. Especially considering it was only twenty degrees outside. She hazarded a glance at Dex, who looked away from her fast, hiding a grin.

"Going on vacation, boss?" she said, hanging up her heavy work coat on the rack in the corner. "Hate to tell you, but the lake's frozen solid until spring. That means no paddle boarding, water skiing, or wake surfing."

"Nah," Owen said good-naturedly. "Got cabin fever is all, Deputy. Now that you're both here, I can hand out today's assignments. DeeDee, I've got you interviewing that actress, Gina Presti, on the film set. Good job on the interview last night, by the way. And Dex, you can go with her and speak with the other gal Levi Harding said he was seeing, find out if she corroborates his alibi. Got it?"

"Yep," they both said in unison.

Walking out together, she and Dex both stopped short at the sight of Stan in the evidence room, whistling to himself as he rearranged boxes. DeeDee raised a brow at Dex then shook her head before continuing out to the parking lot.

"I can drive if you want," she said.

"Sure." Dex climbed into the passenger side of the squad car while DeeDee got behind the wheel. She started the engine and cranked the heat, and they took off.

"What do you think's up with Stan?" Dex asked.

"Ursula. That's what's up. Did you see his neck yesterday?"

"No."

"He had two puncture marks on the side." DeeDee pointed to her own neck, right near her jugular. "My guess is he's under her thrall. Remember that day we went to the morgue and he seemed infatuated with her? Well, looks like she feels the same for him. Now that she's bitten him, he'll stay in his trance-like state indefinitely. I, for one, couldn't be happier."

"It is a lot nicer this way," Dex said, settling into his seat.

They arrived at the movie set a short while later, and DeeDee headed for the dressing rooms inside the mansion while Dex went in search of the actress involved with Levi Harding. Given the dilapidated condition of the rest of the mansion, the dressing room was nice enough, she supposed. Gina had her own little table set up off to one side, and a mirror. Makeup was set out neatly on the tabletop, including several tubes of lipstick. None of them, however, matched the shade of coral from the napkin found at Rockwood's house.

Gina walked in moments later and shook DeeDee's hand. "You must be from the sheriff's office. I'm Gina Presti."

"Nice to meet you, ma'am. I'm Deputy Clawson. I'd like to ask you a few questions if you have time."

"Sure. I'm not on call for another half hour." She took a seat on the small stool in front of her table. "What would you like to know?"

"Were you seeing Tucker Rockwood behind his wife's back?"

The actress blanched, her expression pained. "Wow. You don't waste any time, do you, Deputy?"

"Sorry. But I need a yes-or-no answer, ma'am."

"Yes," Gina said. "But you must understand. Poor Tucker was trapped in that loveless marriage, and his wife, Laura, was such a cold fish." Gina sniffed. "I wouldn't be surprised if she killed him."

"We've already investigated that angle, ma'am. Laura Rockwood's alibi was that the two of you were at the local yoga studio at the time of her husband's death. That *is* where you were on Tuesday night, correct?"

Gina sighed and looked away, her posture sagging. "Yes. Regrettably. I still find it hard to believe Laura didn't have something to do with Tucker's death, though. If anyone had motive to kill him, it was her."

DeeDee pulled out her notebook and jotted down Gina's comments then moved on. "What were you doing prior to arriving at the yoga class and directly after the class ended?"

"I was here on set, in my trailer on RV alley."

"RV alley?"

"Yes, it's a whole row of RVs set up on the perimeter of the movie set for the actors and actresses to live in while they're filming."

"Can anyone else verify your whereabouts?"

"Well, I suppose Johnny could."

"Who's Johnny?" DeeDee frowned.

"Johnny Johnson, the assistant director. He came to give me the dailies from the footage we'd shot on Monday around five on Tuesday morning." Gina shrugged. "These small acting gigs don't pay a lot, so I make some extra money by helping upload footage for the editors and making sure everything's recorded properly."

A man's voice bellowed from outside the dressing room door, yelling for fireworks from the pyrotechnic experts for an important scene. DeeDee glanced from the door to Gina. "Who's that?"

"That's Johnny."

DeeDee scowled, her extra-sensitive werewolf hearing still ringing from the noise. "Does he always yell?"

"Unfortunately, yes." Gina gave her an apologetic smile.

"Did he and Tucker Rockwood ever fight?"

"Oh yeah. All the time. Tucker was a prima donna. Especially lately because he thought he should get paid more," Gina said. "It got so bad, he even refused to film some scenes."

"Huh." DeeDee made more notes. "Would that anger Johnson enough to kill him?"

"Johnny? A killer? No way." Costume maven Sheila fluttered in with a gown for Gina and butted into their conversation. "For all his bluster, the guy's a wimp. Wouldn't hurt a flea. Besides, if anything, Tucker Rockwood's death has been good for business."

"I'm sorry?" DeeDee asked, confused. "How is that possible?"

"Like this." Shelia pulled out her phone and showed her the movie's Facebook page. "Look at the number of hits we've gotten since Tucker's death. It's at least triple what it was before. Way more people are interested in the movie now because of his death."

"But won't the film get cancelled with the leading star gone?" If she lived to be a thousand, DeeDee would never understand show business. "They can't finish without Tucker, right?"

"Wrong." Sheila clicked off her phone and grinned. "Caine Hunter had already planned to cut some of Rockwood's scenes once he'd started making a fuss. Plus, we filmed many of the key scenes out of sequence, so Tucker already had those done. I'd guess Caine and Johnny will just find a way to shoot around him, or maybe use a body double." Sheila winked. "So yeah. Even though poor old Tucker Rockwood's gone, the show must go on, right?"

CHAPTER 17

By the time she'd finished her interview with Gina, DeeDee's head was pounding, and her ears still hurt. She walked outside and stood on the porch, appreciating for once the cold slap of wind on her face. Her list of suspects grew shorter and shorter by the day.

Which was good.

Except the one person she most wanted to cross off her list was still on there.

Caine Hunter.

As much as she hated to talk to him again, she didn't have much choice. Especially after what Sheila had told her. The fact Caine had worked around the possibility of Tucker's disappearance was a little too convenient for her taste.

Dex was still interviewing Harding's love interest, so she interrupted long enough to let him know she was running over to the Hunter estate again to ask the director a few questions.

"I'll be back in about an hour to pick you up, buddy."

He nodded.

Driving usually relaxed her, but all the way back to Caine's majestic estate, DeeDee couldn't seem to shake the coiling tension inside her. She seriously had to get over this thing she had for the sexy director. Most likely, Caine Hunter knew exactly the effect he had on her and was using it to keep her distracted and throw her off the scent of the real killer.

Gripping the wheel tightly, she growled. That was unacceptable.

Her attraction to him had clouded her judgment. It was time to put a stop to it before her case was compromised. In truth, Caine had access to the props, he had secrets in his background, and he had motive. The only thing he didn't have was the rat poison, at least that DeeDee had found.

Yet.

She buzzed in at the gate to Caine's home and spoke to uppity Jarvis again. Then she sped to the house and jammed the cruiser into park.

It was time to face this whole mess head on and get past it once and for all.

Jarvis bowed as he answered the front door, and DeeDee charged past him without waiting for his invitation this time. "I need to speak with Mr. Hunter immediately."

Caine walked into the foyer from the great room, looking both surprised and amused. "What are you doing here, DeeDee?"

"That's Deputy Clawson to you. Where were you Tuesday around four a.m.?"

His smile faltered. "I was here, at home. My sister and Jarvis can verify my whereabouts."

"Right." She crossed her arms. "Do you have any other way of proving it?"

"Do I need one?" Caine mimicked her defensive posture and frowned. "What happened to a person being innocent until proven guilty?"

DeeDee's gut instincts went on high alert. *Spoken like a man who has something to hide.* "Did you know advanced ticket sales for your film increased since Tucker's death? And hits to your social media accounts have skyrocketed. Is that why you did it? Kill Rockwood to create buzz for your movie and make more money?"

"Whoa." Caine held up his hands and backed away. "I didn't kill anybody. That's crazy. I told you, Tucker's death didn't help me at all. Not in the long run, because now I won't have him to star in the sequel."

A sneeze tickled DeeDee's nose, and her arms started to itch. She looked up to see a sprig of mistletoe hung in the doorway above Caine's head. It wasn't exactly the same species Raine had told her about, but it was close enough. Gaze narrowed, DeeDee stalked over to him. "Do you have rat poison on the premises?"

"I don't know. I don't handle that stuff." Caine frowned. "Why?"

She strode through the gorgeous great room and into the sparkling kitchen, stopping before the locked door and pointing at it. "What's in here?"

Caine trailed behind her, his expression guarded. "Nothing you need to see."

"Is that so?" Anger bubbled hot in her bloodstream. He was so pompous, so self-righteous, so…so… *Argh.* "I can come back with a warrant if you want to do this the hard way."

Grumbling under his breath, Caine pulled a key from the drawer beside him then handed it to her. DeeDee snatched it from his fingers.

"Wait!" Caine said as the lock clicked open.

But she was through with waiting. She yanked the door open and stuck her head inside. It turned out the door led to another, smaller room. Stunned, DeeDee walked into the sunny space, staring all around, unable to believe what she saw. A sewing table, complete with an array of fine threads and muslins. A half-finished embroidery piece on a large hoop stand. Walls lined with framed needlework pieces, many of them familiar. Familiar because they were the same ones she'd seen at night on her laptop, when she'd exchanged photos with…

She turned, feeling slightly light-headed as she stared at Caine. "These… I know this work. Is it Carletta?"

Caine looked at the floor, his cheeks turning crimson. "Not exactly."

DeeDee frowned. "What do you mean 'not exactly'? This work is beautiful. Why would she be embarrassed…"

Caine grinned sheepishly.

"It's not her work, is it?"

Caine shook his head.

"*You're* Threads99?"

Caine's brows rose in surprise. "I am. But how did you know?"

"Because I'm Stitches." Heat flared from her cheeks, and her knees felt weak, and if she didn't get out of that room right now, DeeDee thought she might pass out. She shoved past Caine into the kitchen and clutched onto the granite island to stay upright. "I can't believe this."

"Please don't tell anyone," Caine said, taking the key from her and securing the door to his secret room once more. "It's not exactly a manly hobby, especially for a werewolf."

"But your work is beautiful," she said, shocked to find her voice breathy and shaken. "And I don't think it's unmanly. It's cool. It shows you have a gentler side too."

A side her father certainly never had. Most likely a side her future MacPherson husband wouldn't have either. Knowing this secret about Caine Hunter made DeeDee like him even more.

"Wait a minute. You couldn't have killed Tucker Rookwood." She pulled her phone out and scrolled quickly through her screens.

"I've told you that."

"No, look. Here's proof." She showed him the screen with their forum conversation the night Tucker was killed. It was time-stamped, their conversation taking place between three and four thirty a.m. Tuesday morning. "I'm your alibi. We were in the chat room together when the victim was killed. I still don't understand why you're so intent on finding Rockwood's murderer, though."

"Because I feel responsible. His body was found on my movie set, and he was working for me at the time. Why wouldn't I—"

"Want to find the person responsible?" DeeDee said, finishing his sentence.

They stared at each other across the span of a few inches. Completing each other's thoughts was something only soul mates did. But she couldn't be Caine's soul mate. She was destined to marry another. Even if her identifying with his feelings of responsibility seemed to draw the cord connecting them ever tighter.

While she stared at him, dazed, Caine leaned in and brushed his mouth softly over hers, once, twice, before capturing her lips with his. Emotions—want, need, fear, elation—stormed through DeeDee like a hurricane. So many feelings that she wanted to hold Caine tight and never let him go.

Then, as fast as the kiss had started, he pulled away. "Listen, DeeDee. I—"

The clearing of a throat had them stepping apart fast.

Carletta stood in the doorway, glaring at them.

Mortified, DeeDee couldn't meet the other woman's gaze. She was in uniform, on duty, here on a case. She had no business kissing anyone, especially Caine Hunter. Flustered, she backed out of the kitchen and into the great room. "I need to go."

CAINE STARTED after DeeDee but was stopped by his sister's hand on his arm.

"Let her go, brother," she said. "She needs some distance."

"But…" He blinked, unable to believe what had happened.

"She completed your sentence. Yes, I heard." Carletta leaned against the side of the island. "Do you sense her emotions too?"

He shook his head, still fuzzy with thoughts of their kiss. The way she'd felt in his arms, the way she'd smelled—like pine and perfection—the way she'd tasted like his every dream come true. "I don't know. Maybe… It's hard to tell."

"That's good. It means you may be perfect for each other," his sister said, the concern in her tone in direct opposition to her encouraging words.

"What's wrong with being well-suited?" Caine asked, frowning.

"I just don't want you to get hurt again, Caine. The fact you haven't told your future wife who you are yet troubles me. I don't want to see you get your heart broken again. You must proceed with caution here, or DeeDee could turn against you forever. And that would not make for a good marriage."

"You're right." He scrubbed his hands over his face. "I need to tell her the truth before things get even more screwed up."

"Well, just don't blurt it out. That's what it looked like you were going to do when I interrupted," Carletta said. "Try using a bit of finesse."

"Finesse?"

"Yes. Make it meaningful to her." She moved around the island to lean in beside him. "DeeDee doesn't strike me as the type to forgive a liar easily. Perhaps you should focus more on how you plan to tell her the truth than on finding Tucker Rockwood's killer. The cops are already searching for the culprit, anyway. Leave it to them."

"I'm not investigating," Caine said, shaking his head. "Not like she thinks, anyway. I'm more focused on making sure DeeDee stays safe when she goes to some of these interviews. There's a dangerous killer on the loose, and she's lead deputy on the case. It's her job to put herself in harm's way. But as her future mate, it's my job to protect her. And I intend to do so, even if it means I have to track down this murderer myself."

CHAPTER 18

*T*roubled and flustered, DeeDee rushed back to headquarters. She called Dex on the way to see if he was ready to be picked up, but he said he was still talking to some of the other cast and crew on set, so she said she'd call him again in another hour. She switched off the Bluetooth in the cruiser then leaned back in her seat. *I kissed Caine Hunter.* Great balls of fire, that was bad. So, so bad. And yet, it had felt easy and natural and so, so good.

Caught up in her thoughts, she drove back to the station on autopilot. She parked the cruiser and headed inside without paying much attention and nearly barreled over Stan along the way. The poor guy looked as distracted as ever, aimlessly wandering down the hall.

Despite her whirling emotions, she couldn't let the poor man make even more of a fool of himself in front of Owen. She grabbed him by the arm and pulled him aside, shaking his shoulders slightly until he focused on her. "Hey. Stan, buddy. Where you going?"

"To the morgue," he said, his words slurred and his grin dopey. "Want to see if there's anything new on the case."

"Yeah, right." She poked her head into a nearby storage room, saw it was empty, then shoved Stan inside. "Okay, buddy. Before you go back to the morgue, I need you to rearrange and straighten all the supplies in here. Got it?"

Stan frowned slightly then nodded. "Yep."

"Great. I'll come back and check on you in a bit." She closed the door and locked it from the outside then headed into the office. Owen looked unusually perturbed for such a normally laid-back guy. DeeDee took off her coat then walked over to his desk. "Everything okay, boss?"

"Have you seen Agent Judge anywhere? I swear that guy's never at his desk."

She glanced in the direction of the storage room then swallowed hard. Owen was still totally oblivious to all the paranormal activity happening under his nose, and she wasn't about to tell him otherwise. "Actually, I saw him in the hall. He said he was on his way back to the morgue to check on developments in the Rockwood case."

"Yeah?" Owen scoffed. "He seems to be spending an inordinate amount of time there these days. I've got to say, I'm disappointed in Stan. From what I'd heard from the FBI, I expected him to be a good, hardworking investigator, but so far, all he's been is a slacker."

As much as DeeDee preferred the new and improved —and less nosy—Stan, she didn't want to see the guy's reputation go down in flames because of his infatuation with a vampire either. Besides, if she and Dex continued to keep up their fine work at deceiving him, Stan's hubris would do that all on its own. She shrugged. "I don't know. I kind of like a mellower Stan."

"Seriously?" Owen shook his head. "Right now, that guy's about as useful as a pig at a barn dance." He sat forward and waved her closer and handed her the Rockwood file. "But I guess we really don't need him anyway. Between you, me, and Dex, we'll get this murder solved easy-peasy. What'd you find out at the movie lot, Deputy?"

She told him about her interview with Gina Presti and how Dex was still there talking to some other members of the crew. Finally, she came out with her bombshell. "Caine Hunter isn't the killer."

Owen raised a brow at her abrupt announcement. "How do you know?"

"I went to his place after I talked with Gina. I had a few more questions about the increase in exposure for the movie since Tucker's death. Turns out Caine has an airtight alibi for Tuesday night, so we can cross him off our list." DeeDee took a deep breath, knowing her words were rushed and she was babbling, but she couldn't seem to help it. Things between her and Caine were still too new, too confusing, too tender. She just prayed Owen wouldn't notice her agitation or ask for further clarification.

No such luck.

"What exactly is this alibi of his, Deputy?"

"Well, uh, he was, um…" *Crap, crap, crap.* It wasn't as if she could come out and say the guy was online with her in an embroidery chat room. No way would Owen buy that. But she didn't want to outright lie either—that went against her moral fiber. So she compromised. "He was participating in a remote-link conference, which I've verified."

Owen scrunched his nose. "What the heck is *that*?"

DeeDee opened her mouth to answer but was saved at the last minute by Dex walking in.

He shook the snow from his dark hair then pounded his boots on the rug by the door. She swiveled to face him. "How'd you get back here, Dex?"

Dex shrugged off his coat and hung it up. "Rode with some of the sound crew. They were making a coffee run and offered to drop me off. Thought I'd save you the trip since the roads are getting kind of dicey."

"Aw, thanks." DeeDee smiled as he pulled up a chair beside hers in front of Owen's desk. "We were discussing my interview with Gina Presti," she said, hoping to steer the conversation away from Caine and his alibi. "Laura Rockwood had told me Tucker was fooling around on her with Gina, and Gina confirmed it. But then Levi Harding mentioned yet another blonde he'd seen with Tucker, which means he could've been a serial womanizer. Anyway, both Gina Presti and Laura Rockwood have verified alibis for the night of the murder, and Levi said he saw Gina at a different location at the time Tucker was with this second, mystery blonde, which takes her even farther out of the realm of contention. I have taken that information with a grain of salt, though, because Harding and Rockwood were adversaries, so it's possible Levi's using this second blond girlfriend to throw us off his scent as a possible suspect for the murder."

"Sorry, Deputy, but I beg to differ." Dex stretched out his long legs in front of him. "I talked to the actress Harding's dating on the film set, and she verified what Levi told us. Tucker *was* with another blonde, not Gina."

"You believe her?" Owen asked.

"I do." Dex thumped his notepad on his leg. "She didn't show any signs of deception. I say we focus on Caine Hunter. From what several members of the crew told me, his production company stands to make a sizable profit from Rockwood's death, what with all the extra publicity and the boost of the movie on social media."

"No. It's not Caine," DeeDee said, staring down at her own notes. "When I went back over to talk to him this afternoon, he brought up another good point. He won't benefit from Tucker's death in the long run because now he's got no star for his sequel. Plus, he's got an alibi I've verified."

Owen sighed and sat back, placing his sneakered feet

onto his desk. At least he'd changed out of those hideous neon-striped board shorts from earlier and now sported his usual beige khakis. "What about that sister of his?" he asked. "Carletta? She's blond and quite attractive. Maybe she's Tucker's new diversion on the side?"

"Could be." Dex shrugged. "That might explain why Caine Hunter keeps turning up at all our crime scenes too, claiming to be investigating. Perhaps he's trying to cover for his sister."

As much as DeeDee wanted to deny that, she couldn't. In fact, her thoughts had run in the same direction earlier. Caine would be upset if it turned out to be Carletta, but honestly, she was just glad it wasn't him. Still, could she consider a relationship with a guy who'd lie and cheat to keep his murdering sibling out of jail? Such acts would mean Caine was still breaking the law, which was unacceptable in her book—no way around it. In the end, she supposed, it didn't matter, anyway, since there could never be anything more than friendship between her and Caine Hunter.

Owen exhaled and clasped his hands atop his belly. "Levi Harding says he saw them together. Do you think he'd recognize Carletta from a photo? There must be some online from the society pages or something we could use to show him, right?"

"I'll look, boss." She and Dex returned to their desks, and DeeDee switched on her computer. Within five minutes, she had more pictures of Carletta Hunter than she could ever have wished for. She selected a headshot and printed it out then checked her watch. It was near four thirty now.

With luck, Levi Harding would still be on duty at the protest line. She unlocked the storage room, leaving the door closed. Had Stan been in there quietly straightening supplies the whole time? She didn't have time to deal with him right now. He could find his own way out. She continued down the hall and popped into Owen's office again to show him the picture she'd found.

"Good," he said. "Go back to Levi Harding and see if this jogs his memory. While you're gone, I'll have Dex call in some favors from his FBI resources to dig into her background a bit more."

CHAPTER 19

*B*y the time DeeDee made it back to the Crenshaw mansion, Levi was indeed still there. She parked her car near the gates then rushed over to where he stood, huddled behind his large protest sign proclaiming Vamps Are Tramps.

"Mr. Harding," DeeDee said, bracing inside her thick brown coat against the bitter cold. "I have a photo here of a woman we think might have been the woman you saw with Tucker that night in the carriage house. Would you mind looking at it, please?"

"Yeah, sure," he said from behind the thick wool scarf wrapped around the bottom of his face. "Let me see."

DeeDee held out the photo of Carletta Hunter she'd printed off the Internet. "Is this her?"

Harding squinted at the picture then cocked his head. "Nah. That's not her. In fact, I just saw the other blonde go onto the movie set not too long ago. I recognized her hat. Should've known it was her that morning."

"Why is that?" She frowned as she shoved the photo back into her pocket.

"The blonde Tucker was with that night was the same woman who screamed and carried on when they found his body."

Eyes wide, DeeDee pulled out her notebook once more and flipped back through the copious notes she'd taken that first day on the crime scene. Luckily, she'd written down all the names of the crowd that day. "Is it Alissa Snow?"

"Yep." Levi Harding nodded. "That's her name."

"And you said she just arrived on set? Any idea where she might be now?"

"She's one of the main leads today, and I think they're filming inside the house due to the cold. I'd try in there."

"Thanks." DeeDee flashed her badge to the guards again, though by now they all had to know who she was. Still, protocol was protocol. Now wasn't the time to slip up, not with them finally getting closer to who might've killed Tucker Rockwood. She walked up the rickety front steps of the mansion to the old wraparound porch then wedged her way inside the crowded front parlor of the house. Cameras and crew and equipment were everywhere, and bright lights shone from all four corners of the space, helping to heat the otherwise chilly air. In the middle of it all stood the blonde, Alissa Snow, along with another actor DeeDee didn't recognize. And dang if she wasn't wearing the same coral lipstick they'd found on the napkin in Tucker Rockwood's pocket.

DeeDee sighed and crossed her arms. It was entirely possible Ms. Snow's hysterical antics around Tucker's body had been just a show to cover up the fact she was the real killer. Being an actress certainly meant Ms. Snow had the skills to create quite a distraction.

"Cut!" Johnny Johnson yelled at last, and DeeDee made a beeline for Alissa.

"Ms. Snow? I'm Deputy Clawson of the Silver Hollow Sheriff's Department, and I wondered if I might ask you a few questions."

"Oh." Alissa frowned as several dressers and makeup people primped her hair and fussed with her clothes. "I guess."

"Great. How well did you know Tucker Rockwood?"

"Um, we worked together on the movie, of course, and…"

"I know you were intimately involved with him, Ms. Snow. I have witnesses."

Several of the dressers looked up at the statement, and Alissa's cheeks flushed bright red. She excused herself and pulled DeeDee off to a more private corner of the set. "Okay, fine. Yes, Tucker and I were fooling around a bit, but we were in love."

"And you were aware he was a married man?"

"Yes, but it was a loveless marriage. In fact, Tucker told me he was going to leave his wife and marry me someday."

She snorted. That would make Alissa at least third on the list of women Rockwood had promised that to. "I'm sorry to say you weren't the only other mistress he had, Ms. Snow. Is it possible you found out about his other liaisons and became so angry you lashed out at him, maybe even killed him?"

"No!" Alissa gasped, her hand fluttering around her mouth in true outraged starlet fashion. "I loved Tucker. I did. And he loved me. There's no way I would ever hurt him, let alone kill him. Never."

Given the overacting taking place on the part of Alissa Snow, either the woman was dumb enough to believe Tucker had cared about her, or she was delusional. Or both. DeeDee tried out a different theory instead. "Okay. Maybe Rockwood *was* going to leave his wife, but perhaps he wasn't doing it fast enough for your liking and you killed him in a fit of passion."

Even as she said it, though, the words didn't ring true. The forensic reports showed Tucker had been poisoned, which would indicate the murder had been premeditated, not a rash act. Of course, Alissa here could have been one of those *Fatal Attraction*-type women. With all the Hollywood types in this case, it was hard to apply normal logic to them.

She reviewed her notes again. "Did you give Tucker Rockwood a napkin from The Coffee Connection with your lipstick print on it?"

"Yes." Alissa's expression clouded over and her eyes welled with tears. "He hadn't been feeling well, and I gave it to him as a kiss to carry with him to chase away the sickness when I wasn't around."

DeeDee managed to suppress her gag reflex at the sticky sweetness of it all. She pulled out a pen and flipped to a new blank page in her notepad. "Right. And where were you early Tuesday morning between three forty and four seventeen a.m.?"

"Filming a sunrise scene over at the mausoleum in the small family graveyard near the back of the property. Dozens of other people were there too. They can attest to my location."

"And you were there the entire time?" DeeDee asked, not looking up from her paper. It was easier to stay objective and focused without getting distracted by the actress's wild gestures and exaggerated expressions.

"Yes. The only time I left was to get the wooden dolly. But I wasn't alone. Jules walked over to the props trailer with me since we weren't in the next scene they were shooting."

"I'm assuming this Jules person is another actor in the film?" she asked.

"Of course. Jules Mannington. He's quite talented. Handsome too. He'll be a big star someday. Maybe even as big as Tucker."

DeeDee scribbled more notes. Perhaps this Jules Mannington got tired of waiting for his shot at the spotlight and decided to speed things along by getting Tucker Rockwood out of the way. Maybe he'd even gotten Alissa Snow here to help him. She tapped the tip of her pen against her pad. "And this Jules can verify your whereabouts?"

"Sure."

"Great." It seemed everyone was covering for everyone else on this set. "What time would you say the two of you went to get this dolly?"

Alissa frowned, her brows drawing together in deep concentration. "Around three thirty, I think. You can check with Johnny to be exact. All our film takes are time-stamped. Anyway, after we went and got the dolly, Jules and I had to go right back to film another scene. It was a busy night, and we didn't get done until nearly seven that morning. That's when we heard all the commotion…"

"Okay. So you and this Jules went to get the dolly around three thirty and then came right back to start filming again and stayed on the set then until the body was found. Is that correct?"

"Yep."

Except that didn't make any sense. DeeDee already knew from Tucker's FitBit record that the body had been moved between three forty and four seventeen, and their crime scene technicians had proven that wooden dolly had transported the body. "What happened to the dolly while you and Jules filmed your scene?"

"Not sure," Alissa said. "Running props around the set isn't my usual job. I've got more important things to do. I assume it stayed there on set until someone on the crew returned it to the props trailer."

"So you didn't notice if it was still sitting around when you left then?"

"No. Of course not." More tears and sniffles. "With Tucker's death, I was totally devastated. Why would I notice where a stupid cart was when the man I loved was dead?"

DeeDee waited until the actress's sobs calmed to a few hiccupping gasps, then continued. If they gave out Oscars for being drama queens, this gal should have won one.

Finally, Alissa Snow dabbed her eyes and nose. "Look, if you think I killed Tucker, you're just wrong, Deputy. I loved him, truly, madly, deeply. If there's anyone you should be questioning, it's Tucker's wife. Laura was stalking him, you know? I saw her doing it myself, the day before he died. Found her spying on us outside that coffee shop."

It was possible Alissa was trying to set up Rockwood's widow. DeeDee hadn't quite figured out her plan yet, but she would. "Don't worry, Ms. Snow. We're questioning the widow as well."

"Good." The actress's expression turned stubborn, and she crossed her arms. "And if you don't believe what I just told you, please, ask Jules. He's right over there."

Following the direction in which Alissa pointed, DeeDee spotted a young, dark-haired man of medium build with a dazzling-white smile and dimples that would let him get away with just about anything. She finished with Ms. Snow then made her way to the opposite side of the set, where Jules Mannington was holding court.

"Excuse me." DeeDee squeezed between a flock of crew members and makeup people. "Mr. Mannington, I'm Deputy Clawson of the Silver Hollow—"

"Yeah, I know who you are," Jules said, turning his mega-watt smile on her. "I've seen you and the other detective around the set the past few days. Wondered when you'd get around to questioning me."

"Well, then. Today's your lucky day." She gave the actor a flat stare, letting him know she wasn't impressed with his slick persona. "So Mr. Mannington. I just spoke with your friend Alissa Snow, and I need you to verify a few facts for me."

She went through the same questions with him as she had with Alissa, and darn if he didn't give the same exact answers. DeeDee's gut told her these two might be lying, but then again, she tended to be biased when it came to anything Hollywood. Just look at how she'd suspected poor Caine when all along he'd been innocent. Not only that, but he'd also turned out to be her treasured online friend, Threads99. The familiar tingle of awareness started once more in her gut as she remembered their steamy kiss in his kitchen.

She shouldn't be thinking about Caine. Shouldn't be remembering their kiss. It could never work, because she was promised to another. The mustard seed necklace warmed against her skin. But what if there really was a chance...

Nope. DeeDee stepped back and frowned. This was ridiculous. This was getting out of hand. Her fate was sealed. It was better to focus on work. This was her murder investigation, and she needed to stick with the facts and only the facts, leaving her emotions and personal opinions out of it.

And the fact was, the sheriff's department had only released Tucker Rockwood's time of death, not the fact that they knew the time the body was moved. This gave her an advantage. It also meant Alissa Snow was smarter than she let on. By saying she and Jules had retrieved that dolly from the props trailer then left it on the graveyard set gave them an instant out if any of their fingerprints or other DNA evidence turned up on the dolly. And it could also be used as an excuse if anyone had seen her or Jules with the dolly.

Still, no matter how smart this Alissa Snow thought she was, no way would she outsmart DeeDee. She'd worked too hard, been through too much to give up on her case. Now, all she had to do was figure out a way to prove the actress was lying, and she'd be all set.

She went back to her cruiser and pulled out of the driveway to head back into town. It was close enough to five now that she could call it a day. But as she approached a red light, she glanced over and saw Caine Hunter walking into The Coffee Connection.

Before she realized her actions, DeeDee signaled and pulled into the parking lot.

CHAPTER 20

*C*aine glanced out the window of the coffee shop and sighed. *Darn.* He'd thought he'd gotten inside quickly enough to avoid DeeDee seeing him, but he'd been wrong. He watched as she pulled her car in beside his Bentley.

He'd been trailing after her since she'd left his place earlier, despite his sister's warnings to the contrary. No matter how ridiculous or unwanted his help might be, he had an obligation to his future mate, just as he'd told Carletta. She was his responsibility now, and he'd do everything in his power to make sure no harm came to her from this point forward.

His shoulders tensed as he waited for the bell above the door to jangle, though now that their connection was even stronger since that kiss, he didn't need to see DeeDee to know she was close. Still, she never came inside, just sat out in the parking lot, watching him through the window.

It seemed he wasn't the only one doing a little surveillance.

He placed his order, paid, then moved down the line to wait for his coffee.

To distract himself from the zinging awareness jolting through him, even with the windows separating them, Caine went through what he knew about the case so far. He'd discovered Tucker and Gina were fooling around together and that there was also a third woman involved. He'd suspected it was Alissa Snow, though he hadn't confirmed that yet. He also knew Tucker liked to frequent this place with his girlfriends. He'd come here hoping maybe one of the servers might've heard something.

As the line in front of him dwindled, Caine stepped up to the counter and smiled at the cute little barista making his macchiato. He pulled out the two headshots he'd brought with him of Tucker and Gina. When she turned to face him with his coffee in hand, he made his move. "Hi there. I'm Caine Hunter. I'm the producer and director of the movie shooting in town."

The barista returned his smile, a hint of color staining her cheeks. "I know who you are."

"Great." He stirred the whipped cream and caramel into his cup. "Would you possibly have a second to answer a couple questions for me?"

She glanced at the empty register area then shrugged. "Uh, sure."

"Perfect." Caine showed her the picture of Tucker. "Did you see this man in the shop?"

"Yes. He's the actor who got killed, right? Yeah, he came in here a lot," the barista said. "His wife did too."

"Ah, so you knew Laura too?" Caine flashed her another charming smile.

"I did. She was super nice. Always gave us huge tips." She tucked a strand of loose brown hair from her ponytail behind her ear. "I was sad to hear about what happened to him."

Caine sipped his macchiato and leaned his hip against the counter. "How about this woman—did you ever see her in here with Mr. Rockwood?"

He showed her the headshot of Gina Presti.

The barista squinted at the picture. "Yes, I think I saw her in here with him a few times. Why?"

"Did you ever see Tucker Rockwood with other ladies who weren't his wife? Maybe see him get overly friendly with these women?"

The barista hesitated.

"It's okay, you can tell me," Caine said, using his best calming voice, the one he used on set all the time with his overwrought actors and actresses. "It won't go any farther than us."

She nodded, her gaze lowering. "Yeah, I saw them."

"Did he happen to come in with one of these other women on Monday?"

"Yes."

Caine pulled a third headshot from beneath his coat,

this one of Alissa Snow. "Was this the woman you saw with him that day?"

"Yeah," the barista said. "That's her."

"And you're sure it wasn't this woman I showed you before." He placed Gina's picture beside Alissa's. "They're both blond, so it might be easy to confuse them."

"No. It was definitely the second lady. The funny thing is, though, that first lady showed up later in the day too. I remember because she came in with Laura." The barista shrugged. "I thought it was weird, the two of them hanging out together and being all cozy."

Frowning, Caine gathered the pictures and thanked the girl for her help then took a seat at an empty table near the windows so he could keep an eye on DeeDee.

Why the heck would Gina Presti and Laura Rockwood hang out in a coffee shop together? From what he'd heard, the two women couldn't stand each other, unless it was all a ruse to throw people off. And why would they want to do that?

Caine had the disturbing feeling that his future mate could be in far more danger than he'd ever imagined. The connection between them flared brightly, bringing all his alpha protector instincts to the forefront. He downed the rest of his coffee before hazarding another glance out the window.

But when Caine looked out to the parking lot again, DeeDee was gone.

eeDee settled into her booth in The Main Squeeze juice bar and pulled out her cell phone. The fact she'd just wasted twenty minutes of her life staring at the man she'd kissed earlier in the day left her decidedly off-kilter. She wasn't a stalker. In fact, she wasn't the type of woman who chased after men at all. Yet there she'd been, wistfully watching Caine Hunter through The Coffee Connection windows as he'd flirted with a barista.

Envy and embarrassment roiled inside her, preventing her from fully enjoying the tasty Pomegranate Passion drink she'd ordered. It was best to forget all about Caine and the kiss they'd shared and the fact he seemed to affect her as no other man ever had and get back to business.

That was the proper thing to do. The safe thing to do.

She dialed Owen's number then sat back and unzipped her coat while she waited for him to pick up.

"Sheriff Gleason."

"Hey, boss," DeeDee said. "Is Dex there too? If so, you might as well put me on speaker phone so we can get this all out at once."

"Sure, hang on."

Moments later, the sound through the phone line shifted from regular to airplane-hanger mode. The noise of chairs being shuffled across the floor echoed. DeeDee sipped her drink and stared out the window as snow flurries whipped around in the breeze over the Silver Hollow town green across the street from the shop.

"Hey, partner," Dex said at last.

"Hey, buddy." She smiled and pulled out her notebook. "Okay, so I just got done questioning Alissa Snow, and I'm pretty sure we've got ourselves a new top suspect."

"Really?" Owen said. "Why's that?"

"Well, for starters, she was the one who retrieved the dolly from the props trailer."

"Really?" Dex asked.

"Yep. Boss, can you pull up the crime scene technician's report for the wooden dolly and tell me if they found any other DNA evidence linking Alissa Snow to the murder of Tucker Rockwood? Hair or skin or fingerprints."

Owen came back on the line a few moments later. "Nope. The only prints found at the crime scene were the wife's on Tucker's personal effects—his FitBit and his wallet—but that's not unusual since they were married."

"What about on the dolly itself?" DeeDee asked.

"That thing was a mess of prints. Seems just about everybody and their brother used it. They did find epithelial cells matching Rockwood's DNA, so it was definitely used to transport his body."

"Shoot." She frowned and sat back. She'd thought they'd find at least some hair or fingerprints linking Alissa to that stupid dolly. She sighed, staring down at her notes while Owen and Dex chatted between themselves. She'd written the words "time stamp" in bold. Alissa had said all the scenes they filmed for the movie were time-stamped. If she had killed Tucker Rockwood, then that would mean Alissa would've somehow had to tamper with the time stamp on the scenes she shot with Jules Mannington. Was that even possible?

DeeDee flipped back to a few days earlier in her notes. Gina Presti had said she helped the assistant director by uploading the dailies for the editorial team. Gina mentioned the assistant director had brought her a batch of film to upload early Tuesday morning, the day Tucker Rockwood's body had been found. Maybe Gina would be able to tell her more about the time stamps.

"Hey, boss?" she said after taking a long sip of her Pomegranate Passion. "I'm going to head back over to the movie set before the end of my shift. I've got a few more questions for Gina Presti."

"Be careful, Deputy." Owen said. "I'll see you in the morning."

"Bye, DeeDee," Dex said.

"See ya later."

She ended the call then bundled up again before heading back out to the cruiser.

GINA ANSWERED the door on her RV, her expression surprised. "Deputy Clawson?"

"Hello again." DeeDee gave her a polite smile. "May I come in? I've just got a couple more questions for you."

"Oh, uh..." Gina glanced into the trailer then back at her. "Okay, I guess. I was just on my way over to the set to work, though, so it'll have to be fast."

"Sure." She climbed the steps into the trailer. It was nice, fully appointed and cozy. Fine for temporary lodgings on a film set but way too cramped to be comfortable for long-term living otherwise. She took a seat at the booth opposite the kitchenette area, noticing the expensive Louis Vuitton handbag on the opposite seat. Gina fussed with a blender on the counter and set some dirty dishes in the sink. A few clothes were strewn about too, as if she hadn't had time to clean up in a while. In the living room area, near the front of the RV, sat a gigantic flat-screen TV perched precariously atop a rather wobbly-looking end table.

"What can I help you with, Deputy?" Gina asked, taking a seat across from DeeDee.

"Well, I was wondering about those…" A familiar tickle started in her sinuses, growing stronger and stronger until—*Acccchhhhoooo!*

Great. Another sneezing fit. Her arms and hands itched like crazy as small hives appeared. Mistletoe. There must have been some close. This species must have been the kind she was super allergic to. It was affecting her much more than any other mistletoe she'd been near. She searched for it as she tried asking her question again. "Sorry. One of the actresses mentioned all the film scenes shot are time-stamped. Can those stamps be changed?"

"Oh." Gina pushed a box of tissues across the table toward her. "I suppose they could be. You'd have to have access to the system, though."

"Who would have that kind of access? Any of the actors or actresses? Alissa Snow?"

"I don't think any of the cast would." Gina frowned as DeeDee scratched her hands raw. "Are you okay?"

"Allergies."

DeeDee sneezed again, knocking over a few books and a coffee mug. DeeDee bent to pick them up and spotted the corner of a note sticking out from one of the books. She pulled it out, spotting Tucker Rockwood's distinctive sloping signature across the bottom. She leaned in to read it, but Gina stood and crossed her arms.

"I think you need to leave now, Deputy. I don't like you snooping around my place." Her tone had gone from friendly to confrontational. She reached over and snatched the note away. "Come back with a warrant next time before you start going through my personal things."

DeeDee slid out of the small booth, her thoughts racing. At Laura's house, the mouse on Tucker's computer had been on the left side, meaning Tucker Rockwood was left-handed.

Yet when his body was found, the FitBit was on his left wrist—opposite of what the manufacturer recommended. He should've worn the thing on his right hand, his nondominant side. A fitness buff like Rockwood would surely have known that. In fact, his wife had said he was obsessed with accurately tracking his steps. He didn't seem like the type that would go against what the manufacturer recommended, not to mention that wearing the FitBit on his dominant hand would cause it to get in the way when he was writing or using the computer.

Then there was the note she'd just seen. Tucker's writing slanted to the left, again exactly what you'd expect for a left-handed writer. Her gaze flicked to the huge TV in the living room then the expensive purse on the seat by the table. Gina had come into money. Laura's money.

All the pieces finally clicked.

DeeDee had based her case on the fact Tucker's FitBit recorded movement of his body between three forty and four seventeen. Both Gina and Laura's alibis were based on the fact they'd been in a yoga class during that time and thereby unable to have been the ones that moved Rockwood. They'd even had witnesses to corroborate their stories. But now…

DeeDee remembered that girl at the yoga studio saying that Gina had brought a pie and she never got a taste. That had bugged DeeDee. Who would bring a pie to yoga? But now DeeDee realized the girl never actually saw the pie—all she saw was Gina carrying something carefully held in front of her. As if she didn't want it going up and down… like the movement necessary for a FitBit to track activity.

Slowly, she looked up toward the ceiling right above the sink and spotted a sprig of mistletoe with thin leaves just as she'd seen online. The most poisonous variety. Her hands and arms felt as if they were on fire, and her throat was swelling shut. Pressure built in her sinuses as she tried to reach for her gun, but erupted in another sneezing fit.

Gina seized the opportunity and tackled DeeDee to the floor.

With the trailer being so narrow, there wasn't much room to move or fend off an attack. Still sneezing and sniffling, she managed to cover her face against the other woman's scratching nails. Eyes watering, she squinted at Gina, who now had her hands around DeeDee's throat in a chokehold.

"How did you figure it out?" Gina demanded.

With her allergic reaction now in full swing, breath labored and throat swelling, she managed to force out rough words. "The F-FitBit. It was o-on the wrong wrist. Tucker's l-left-handed. S-Should've been o-on his r-right."

DeeDee's frazzled mind tossed up more facts. Owen had said Laura Rockwood's fingerprints had been on Tucker's FitBit. Now she knew why. Her vision grew hazy, but she refused to give in to the unconsciousness looming near the edges of her brain. "H-How d-did you k-kill him?"

Gina's expression turned smug. "It was easy, really. Once we decided to get rid of Tucker, Laura slipped the mistletoe into his food and coffee. We weren't sure how much to use to kill him, but she knew it would eventually build up to toxic levels in his bloodstream. After he died, we took off his FitBit and put the body in the back of Laura's pickup truck and drove him to the movie set." She smiled, creepily and coldly. "Do you have any idea how heavy dead bodies are? Way too heavy for two gals like Laura and me to carry, that's for sure. Good thing we found that dolly sitting out on the set. We loaded him up then moved him down to the edge of the property, near the remote swamp so he wouldn't be found right away. Too bad Laura put that stupid FitBit on the wrong wrist, though. We'd been so careful to cover all our tracks."

Making one last attempt to escape, DeeDee bucked hard against Gina. The movement dislodged her assailant, and she gulped in a much-needed breath before shoving the actress hard to the floor and pinning her shoulders to the ground with her knees. "Not as careful as you thought, Ms. Presti. We had movement recorded on Tucker's FitBit during the time he was moved." She frowned, realizing now she'd been duped. "But that's not where the movement came from, was it? You wore the device to the yoga class, didn't you? Is that why you and Laura fought too? To make sure everybody remembered you both being there?"

"Very good, Deputy." Gina chuckled. "We wanted to make sure our visit was unforgettable. Worked too, didn't it? You had no idea it was me and Laura behind it all."

Another sneeze attack threatened, and DeeDee tried to hold it back, but it was too late.

Gina struck again, this time with her fist. She clocked DeeDee's jaw hard, sending her reeling backward. Her head smacked hard on the corner of the cabinets as she fell, white stars blinking in front of her eyes. Before she knew it, she was pinned again, trapped, as Gina sat atop her abdomen. "S-So you and Laura w-were in this together the w-whole time?"

"Of course." Gina squeezed DeeDee's throat again. More white stars flickered before her gaze as her oxygen levels depleted. "Funny, but we actually met when we were both tailing that bastard Tucker. He had issues with women. Couldn't keep his hands off them. When we discovered him with Alissa, Laura and I bonded. We started meeting in that little coffee shop and hatching our plan to take Tucker out. I'd read a story in the paper about a killer's alibi being blown because of a FitBit, and knowing what a fitness nut

Tucker was, we decided to use that technology to our advantage."

DeeDee struggled against her captor's hold, but her strength was waning. She forced herself to focus on more questions, her words emerging more quietly and weakly than she'd intended, biding her time until she could call for help. "What about the p-poison? You mentioned the m-mistletoe. Our ME found p-phoratoxins in Tucker's system. But she also found p-phosphorus. How did y-you know to combine t-the two?"

"Oh, that was all Laura." Gina rested her weight more fully atop DeeDee, making it even harder for her to breathe. "She was a chemist at her father's pharmaceutical company and thought the mistletoe would be the least suspicious poison to use, since it's everywhere during the holidays. If they found it in his system, it would be easy enough to explain away with an accidental ingestion. Except it took way longer than we expected for the levels in his bloodstream to reach toxic levels. He didn't die like we wanted, just kept getting sicker and sicker until she finally decided to mix in a tad of phosphorus with the last dose."

"R-Rat p-poison?" DeeDee managed to squeak out, remembering how Alissa Snow had said Tucker was sick. Had that been from the mistletoe? Probably. And his body was full of it, which was why she'd had that allergic reaction upon finding it.

"No, actually. Fireworks." Gina seemed quite pleased with herself. "Our pyrotechnics crew made it easy enough to obtain. Just grabbed a few from the props trailer when no one was looking. That props master is so lost anyone can take anything at any time."

Dang! Ursula had mentioned fireworks in the list of things that could have phosphorus, but DeeDee had thought it seemed more logical for the killer to have used rat poison. Which it would have been if the murder were under normal circumstances and not on some crazy movie set. "W-What about the s-stake?"

Gina laughed, the sound chock-full of crazy. "We threw that in to confuse you. Figured it would make you suspect one of the protestors."

DeeDee closed her eyes, berating herself now for being so gung-ho to get over here tonight. She should've waited until the morning. Should've brought backup, just in case. She knew better than to not follow protocol. That was what had killed Paige.

Now, it seemed, DeeDee would pay the ultimate price as well for her carelessness.

"Are you having a hard time breathing, Deputy?" Gina asked as she leaned in closer. "Oh, that's too bad."

Acting on pure instinct, DeeDee jerked hard, toppling Gina sideways, and reached for her gun at the same time. Weapon drawn, she stared down at her suspect as pressure built inside her head once more.

No. No sneezing. Not now.

But she couldn't hold it back. In the chaos, they wrestled for the gun, and Gina got hold of the weapon. She scrambled to her feet and aimed, her eyes flat and cold.

"You should have died peacefully when you had the chance, Deputy."

Prepared to take a bullet, DeeDee squeezed her eyes shut and waited. She'd had a good life, done her best to atone for what had happened to Paige all those years ago. Finally found a guy who made her light up inside like a Christmas tree. Caine Hunter. He wasn't her intended, but that kiss had been...*everything*. She'd miss her sister, miss saying goodbye to her dad, even though they never did agree on much. And the guy she was supposed to marry, well...

A loud crack sounded, and DeeDee braced against the pain she expected.

Except the agony never arrived.

Instead, Gina screamed. Brisk wind rushed in along with the scent of pine.

Peeking one eye open, DeeDee spotted a gorgeous blond wolf launching through the open doorway at Gina. The two tumbled to the ground, and the gun dropped to the floor. DeeDee crawled forward to grab it. Her gaze locked with the wolf's, and her pulse stumbled.

She'd know those amber eyes anywhere.

Caine.

Caine Hunter had just saved her life.

Their connection flared supernova brightly, bringing her both comfort and a necessary burst of energy. She stumbled to her feet with the gun in one hand and pulled her cell phone from her pocket and dialed 9-1-1 with the other.

The dispatcher answered, and DeeDee relayed what had happened and her location.

Within minutes, sirens wailed in the distance. Caine's wolf gave DeeDee one last, longing look then took off through the door, disappearing into the night as she cocked her weapon and unclipped the handcuffs from her utility belt, reading Gina Presti her Miranda rights as she rolled the actress over onto her stomach to slap on the cuffs. "You have the right to remain silent. Anything you say can and will be used against you in a court of law."

"What's happening?" Owen shouted, rushing into the trailer with his gun drawn. Dex was hot on his heels.

"Stand down, boss. I've got the suspect secured." DeeDee finished reading Gina her rights then let Dex and Owen take over. Her knees were shaking, and her throat felt sandpaper raw. That stupid mistletoe still hung above the sink, but she wasn't about to touch it. That was evidence in her murder case, and she wanted everything processed by the book to make sure Gina Presti and Laura Rockwood were both punished for their crimes.

Stan stumbled up the steps to the trailer and peered inside, his expression disbelieving. "Was that a giant werewolf I saw running across the movie set?"

DeeDee exchanged a look with Dex then patted Stan on the shoulder on her way outside. "A giant werewolf, buddy? I think you're seeing things."

CHAPTER 22

A few hours later, after they'd gotten both Gina Presti and Laura Rockwood processed and safely behind bars, DeeDee arrived home at last. Her head was still stuffy and throbbing from her allergies, and her arms and hands were red and raw. She hadn't looked in a mirror since that morning, and DeeDee feared she looked even worse than she felt.

Still, even as happy as she was they'd caught their killers—Laura had caved shortly after they'd brought her in for interrogation—she was still beating herself up for not catching that double-cross with the FitBit sooner.

Then there was Caine's heroic rescue.

As she stumbled into her bedroom and slowly peeled her uniform away from her inflamed skin, she couldn't help remembering the utter calm that had come over her at his nearness. The connection between them was good and right and undeniable.

Too bad he wasn't the man she was slated to marry.

She finished undressing then padded into her bathroom and jammed on the shower. While the water heated, she texted her father once more. If only she could talk to him, explain things between her and Caine, maybe by some miracle he wouldn't make her marry a stranger, wouldn't turn to Nia as a replacement.

No response. As usual.

It was for the best, she supposed as she opened the shower door and climbed under the soothing warm spray. No matter what she said, nothing would change her bullheaded father's mind, and honestly, she did understand his reasoning. Merging with the MacPherson pack was important. She just wished her dad would get over his big ego and stop insisting it be one of his daughters who did the marrying to seal the treaty. Yes, he was their pack alpha, but still.

After scrubbing down then rinsing off, DeeDee got out of the shower and toweled dry, realizing she'd forgotten to take off the mustard seed locket. Its weight still hung around her neck, as if reminding her she had one alternative left.

She slumped down on the edge of her bed and stared at the thing. Deep in her heart, DeeDee knew there was no way she could marry this MacPherson guy, not with what she felt for Caine. It wouldn't be right. There was only one way, though, to stop the marriage and not have the responsibility fall on her sister, Nia. Too bad that one way would get her ostracized from the pack and ensure Caine wouldn't want anything to do with her. But marrying MacPherson would be wrong, and at least she could save her sister from the same fate.

In need of a witch's assistance, DeeDee grabbed her cell phone again and dialed Gray Quinn's number. It was late, but he was paranormal and hopefully still awake.

"Hello?" he answered.

"Hey, Gray. It's DeeDee."

"Hey! How are you?"

"I'm good. Listen, I need some help of the magical variety." She explained the situation and how she needed witchy powers to activate the mustard seed. If it could even still be activated. "Do you think you Quinns can help me?"

"We'll sure try. Anything for you, DeeDee. We can't do it at Issy's, though. This is too big. Way too big. We need a high-energy area."

DeeDee's gut clenched. "You mean…"

"Yep, the Tribunal Bar and Grill. I'll call ahead and see if we can use the back room."

The Tribunal was a seedy joint halfway between north and south Silver Hollow. It was loaded with high energy and had a back room kept reserved for special use. It was rarely used. In fact, most paranormals avoided it because it was also rumored to be the place bad paranormals were brought for punishment sentencing. DeeDee had no idea what that entailed—few who had been brought there came back to tell about it. All she knew was it had something to do with a bunch of judges, paranormal penance, and some hefty fines.

But if it was the only place they could do it, she didn't have much of a choice. "I'll meet you there."

"Okay. I'll let my cousins know what's going on too. Sometimes these things take more than one witch."

"Great. Thanks, Gray. I really appreciate it."

She hung up then pulled on a pair of jeans and a sweatshirt, socks, and sneakers. Her muscles were stiff from the fight with Gina, and she had a knot on the back of her head from where she'd collided with the cabinets in the RV. She slicked her damp hair back into a ponytail then pulled on her heavy work coat and headed out to the squad car, feeling tired to her bones but needing to get this whole marriage thing settled once and for all.

Her neighbor, a nosy little old man named Mr. Roberti, was outside, fussing with his Christmas lights, when she went to get in her squad car.

"Where're you off to so late, Deputy?" he called, waving.

"Meeting some friends at The Tribunal," she called back before climbing into the car.

As she slid behind the wheel, her cell phone buzzed with an incoming message.

DeeDee pulled it out and saw it was from Dex, asking if she was okay. He'd seen the werewolf too, she was sure, but she doubted he made the connection between the creature and Caine. Good thing too, since he also knew about her thing for Caine, because they'd discussed it that day in the car.

She started the engine and backed out of the driveway, giving a final wave to Mr. Roberti before shifting into drive and heading toward the restaurant. Her phone screen dimmed then went black, Dex's text unanswered. The ritual ahead, whatever it would be, required her full concentration.

She'd chat with Dex later.

CHAPTER 23

It was nearly ten at night by the time Caine headed to DeeDee's house. After what had happened between them on the movie set and the way her life had been in danger, he'd needed time to get himself calmed down and get his head on straight again.

He was going to tell her the truth. It was time.

She'd be pissed and most likely wouldn't want to go through with the marriage after the way he'd lied to her, but it was the right thing to do. Besides, no matter what their pack rules said, he refused to force her into marrying him. Deep inside, he knew she was his soul mate. He could only pray on some level she knew it too. Maybe then she'd forgive him and they could start again.

His driver pulled up in front of her tiny little bungalow, and he started up the snowy sidewalk to her door, only to be stopped by a voice shouting from the next house over.

"If you're here to see Deputy DeeDee, you just missed her," a little old man with his hands full of Christmas twinkle lights said.

Caine stopped and walked to her neighbor's house instead. "You wouldn't happen to know where she went, would you?"

The little old guy eyed him up and down as if gauging Caine's measure. He easily had a good foot and a half of height on the elderly man, but that didn't stop the elderly man from defending DeeDee. Caine liked him already. He smiled and held out his hand. "My name's Caine Hunter, and I'm a friend of DeeDee's. I only have her best interests at heart. I promise."

"Mr. Roberti," the guy said, shaking Caine's hand with a surprisingly firm grip. Then he narrowed his gaze. "She carries a gun and a Taser, you know, and she's not afraid to use them. You mess with her, you'll regret it."

"Understood, sir." Caine bit back a smile. DeeDee's courage was one of the things he admired most about her. "Do you know where she went?"

The old man sighed and turned back to his tangled Christmas lights. "The Tribunal Restaurant," he said. "Seemed in an awful hurry to get there too."

"Thanks." Caine walked back to his car then waved. "Nice to meet you, Mr. Roberti."

"You too," the old guy called.

Caine got back into his car then gave the driver the location. It seemed an odd place for DeeDee to go this late. He'd driven by the restaurant several times but hadn't ever gone inside. It looked a bit run-down, to be honest.

His cell phone rang, and Caine glanced at the small screen, seeing an incoming call from the detective who worked with DeeDee.

"This is Dex Nolan. Is DeeDee with you?"

"No." He frowned, his concern growing. "I stopped by her house, and her neighbor said she was on her way to a place called The Tribunal. I'm going there now to talk to her."

"Great. Listen, I know we don't know each other that well, but DeeDee seems to care for you a lot, and I don't want her getting hurt."

"What are you talking about?" Caine gripped his phone tighter. The longer the conversation went on, the more his agitation grew. He had a bad feeling about all this. "Is there something going on I should know about?"

"I don't know," Dex said. "You know I'm an FBPI agent. I know you're paranormal, a werewolf, and so is DeeDee. Anyway, my fiancée's a witch. She got a call from one of her cousins asking her to get over to this Tribunal Bar place quickly. Now, like I said, I don't know what's going on exactly, but whenever those cousins get together, mayhem usually ensues."

"Mayhem?" Caine scowled.

"She mentioned something about a mustard seed locket and a spell. Does that mean anything to you?"

His pulse stumbled, stopped, then restarted triple time. His mother had told him the legend when they were kids. Mustard seeds could be used to plant doubt in someone's mind or make them change their decision. If DeeDee had one and was desperate enough to get out of marrying him, she could use it to erase their marriage contract from her father's mind... but if she got caught doing that, the consequences could be unthinkable.

"Can you go any faster?" he urged the driver then returned to his conversation with Dex. "These cousins of your fiancée's. Do they form a coven of their own?"

"Yep." Dex sighed. "Like I said, I don't know what's going on, and I don't want to interfere, but DeeDee cares for you. I know she does. She's scared, though. She told me once her mom gave her that mustard seed locket. I always thought she wore it as a memento, but now, I don't know. I thought maybe you should know, in case you're involved in this somehow. If you care about DeeDee too, you should tell her. She's a good woman and a great cop. But if you hurt her, I swear—"

"I won't hurt her. Ever," Caine said. Dex was the second man who'd defended DeeDee to him that night. He was well aware of how awesome his soul mate was. Now if only he had a chance to tell her, he'd be all set. "I need to go."

He ended the call and leaned forward as the Mercedes raced toward the middle of Silver Hollow. He had no idea what he'd find when he got to this Tribunal place, but he intended to let DeeDee know how he felt before it was too late.

Minutes later, the driver pulled up in front of a small,

dark bar. A red neon sign buzzed and crackled atop the worn steel entrance door, and a rusted-out brown pickup truck was parked near the curb. He got out and told the driver to wait then headed inside, determined to win the woman he loved, no matter the cost.

CHAPTER 24

*D*eeDee sat in the back room of the seedy restaurant and stared at the stained red carpet beneath her feet. Folding chairs were stacked against the walls, making it look as if it was used more for storage than anything else. The front area hadn't been much better—old maple tables, water-marked tile ceiling, the smell of sauerkraut and musty gym shoes. There was a small bar to one side, dimly lit, with three old patrons nursing their whiskeys on a long sticky bar top. They must have been owners, she assumed. Yeah. The Tribunal might be a so-called high-energy zone, as Gray had said, but it wouldn't be ranking on the Michelin Star registry any time soon.

The Quinn cousins were currently bickering about spells and rituals and bad juju.

She already felt hesitant enough about what she was

about to do. She didn't need the wrath of the Quinns to crash down upon her too.

Finally, Issy came over and took a seat. "Are you sure this is what you want?"

"Yeah, I'm sure." What other choice did she have, really? None that she could see.

"Do you know anything about this man you're pledged to marry? Maybe you should at least meet him first. He could be really nice, and once we do this spell, we can't take it back. And from what I hear, it could be something you want to take back."

DeeDee didn't disagree on that, but she had no choice. She didn't relish what would happen to her once she refused to marry MacPherson after using the mustard seed to plant the idea not to marry Nia off to the MacPherson clan in her father's head. She would be ostracized. Her family and wolf friends would shun her, and she'd be destined to run alone and not frolic with the pack ever again. At least she would save Nia—that was one saving grace. "No, I've not met him. I've tried contacting my dad so many times I've lost count, but he's on his honeymoon and won't answer my calls or texts, so I'm desperate. All I know is his last name is MacPherson and he's due to become alpha once his father passes. From what I've heard through werewolf channels, his pack is pretty prominent and—"

"Ah!" One of the three older men from out front entered the back room from the long dark hallway. The other two elders walked in behind him, one smoking a large cigar. The first elder turned and spoke to another figure approaching down the hall. "Is this the one you're willing to sacrifice for?"

Caine walked into the room, and the world seemed to come to a standstill. "Yes," he said, his eyes never leaving hers as he bowed before the three elders. "I will take her under my protection and take the punishment for her actions."

Stunned, DeeDee pushed to her feet. "Caine, what are you doing here?"

He'd already sacrificed himself for her once, by tackling Gina to the ground in the RV. She couldn't let him do it again. It went against everything she stood for. She was a law enforcement officer, the protector of the people, the one who'd sworn to put her life on the line for others. Still, she could not stop the tiny spark of hope that he was willing to go that far to win her love. Unfortunately, fear soon doused it. Fear he would be punished for his bravery. After all, she was destined to marry a MacPherson. If word got out about what Caine was doing, it could cause severe repercussions for Caine, and she'd hate to see him hurt because of her.

A voice from behind her jarred her from her whirling thoughts. "DeeDee?"

She spun fast to see her father. Her already racing pulse zoomed faster. She took a step back. Something was wrong. "Dad?"

"I'm sorry it took me so long to answer." He stepped

out of the shadows along the wall. "I've been trying to text you, but service was spotty."

"I don't understand." She clutched the edge of a nearby table to steady her trembling hands, the weird tingle of destiny rushing over DeeDee like a tsunami. "I thought you were still on your honeymoon."

"I was. But when I realized I'd forgotten to set up an introductory meeting between you and your new husband, I rushed home to remedy the situation." He winced. "With all my own wedding preparations, I forgot. Looks like I didn't have to worry, though, since he's already here."

"Huh?" A quick glance around the room showed all the same occupants as before—the Quinns, the Tribunal, her, Caine, her dad. "I'm sorry, I don't get it. My mate can't be here. I know all these people and..." Her voice trailed off as realization dawned. Breath hitched, DeeDee turned slowly to face Caine Hunter. "It's you. You're the man I'm supposed to marry."

Caine at least had the decency to look sheepish. Her father, on the other hand, sounded quite pleased with himself. "Yep. He's Caine MacPherson. He's due to inherit leadership from his father someday. What a fine pair you two will make."

The adrenaline sizzling in her blood slowly ignited into pure anger. Her dad talked about them as though they were nothing but livestock, nothing but playing chips to be bartered and traded at his will and discretion.

She shifted her glare from her father back to Caine again.

"I'm so sorry, DeeDee." He held his hands up in surrender. "I wanted to tell you who I was right away. But then we got off on the wrong foot because my movie set kept getting reported and you came out to investigate and—"

"Just save it, okay?" She stepped forward, poking him in the chest with her finger. "This whole time, you could've pulled me aside and told me the truth about who you were and why you were here, but you didn't. Instead, you lied." She advanced again, taking a step forward for every one he took backward until he smacked into the wall. "Forget it. I'm done listening to you, Caine Hunter or MacPherson or whatever the heck your name is." She rose on tiptoe, putting them nose to nose. "And I wouldn't marry you if you were the last werewolf on earth!"

With that, DeeDee stormed out of The Tribunal. She was through with love, through with lies, and most of all —through with Caine MacPherson.

CHAPTER 25

*D*eeDee sat in the comfy chair in her living room, doing her best to finish a particularly intricate section of her appaloosa embroidery pattern. Two days had passed since the blowout with Caine at the Tribunal. Two depressing, confusing, thoroughly vexing days.

She tried yet again to make a French knot, failed completely, and ended up tearing the whole stitch out and starting again. It didn't help that her vision kept blurring, not because of tears, because she refused to cry about what had happened with her father and Caine and all the lies and deception. Nope. She most definitely wasn't crying. It was eyestrain. That was all.

Sniffling, DeeDee tried to start a new stitch, but her heart just wasn't in it.

With a sigh, she set the embroidery piece aside and leaned her head back against the chair. Christmas was just a few days away, and crime was even slower than usual in Silver Hollow. Because of that, and because Owen said she deserved a break after solving the Tucker Rockwood case, he'd given her the holidays off. Normally, DeeDee would've been thrilled to sleep in and get stuff done around her house, but now all she could seem to do was sit around and brood about how screwed up her life was at present.

She'd run through that final confrontation with Caine in her mind until she felt sick, and yet she still couldn't stop thinking about him. Worst of all, she couldn't even get online and discuss her miserable situation with her best friend, Threads99, because yeah—Threads was Caine. Talk about a mess.

Then there was the undeniable ache around her heart that had only intensified since she'd walked out on Caine. She'd long since admitted to herself she loved him, regardless of him not telling her the truth about who he was. The problem was, she wasn't sure she could forgive and forget his betrayal. And once she officially refused to marry him, things would get a lot worse for her.

A knock at the front door jolted her out of her pity party, and DeeDee got up to see who it was. Peeking out the curtains of a nearby window, she spotted Caine's sister, Carletta, on the porch. *Oh, crap.* Of course, the woman looked immaculate as usual, while she looked like a hot mess. She did her best to straighten her rumpled sweatpants and T-shirt then wiped her face and pinched her cheeks to give them some color. Finally, she straightened her ponytail then took a deep breath for courage before opening the door a crack.

Carletta gave her a kind smile. "Hello, DeeDee."

"If you're here because Caine sent you to persuade me to marry him, don't bother." She rubbed her hand under her nose. "I'm through listening to his lies."

"My brother doesn't know I came," she said, peering through the two-inch-wide opening. "Caine would be extremely upset if he knew I was here, but there's something I need to show you."

Curiosity got the better of her, and slowly, DeeDee opened the door. Her small home wasn't nearly as grand as Caine's enormous estate, and she hadn't exactly felt like cleaning the past couple of days. She cleared mail and newspapers off the sofa and stacked them on the nearby coffee table so her guest would have somewhere to sit. "Sorry it's such a mess."

Carletta perched with regal grace on the edge of a sofa cushion then removed a document from her expensive designer handbag. "Here. This is what I wanted you to see."

It looked like a letter.

DeeDee took it over to her comfy chair and held it beneath the lamp. Yep. It was handwritten in Caine's distinctive scrawl. The date on the top was several months prior, shortly after he'd first come to Silver Hollow. Down near the bottom was another date, stamped this time, along with a notary mark and initials.

She met Carletta's gaze. "This is to the Canine Convention."

"Yes." She nodded, her platinum-blond hair shimmering in the light. "My brother doesn't know I asked for a copy of the official document."

The contents of the letter were even more surprising. In fact, the longer DeeDee read, the more her disbelief grew. "I don't understand. This says Caine took full responsibility for the marriage treaty failing. But how could he have known that would happen all those months before?"

"He didn't." Carletta's smile turned sad. "He wanted to give you a way out, DeeDee, in case things didn't go as planned. You see, despite my brother's polished, tough exterior, he's quite gentle and kind and thoughtful on the inside. In fact, he's fought against his playboy image his whole life. Especially after what happened with Brenda, his first girlfriend."

"What happened?" DeeDee asked, unable to help herself.

"She treated him horribly, very selfish and greedy. Turns out she only wanted him because he was going to be pack alpha someday." Carletta shook her head and frowned. "She never deserved my brother. When she left him, Caine was heartbroken and didn't trust anyone again for a very long time. He thought the only reason a woman would want to be with him was for his money, his power, his prestige." She shrugged. "Then he met you and found out you were to be his mate. My brother wrote that letter so you would never be forced to marry him. He only wants a mate who will be his true love." Carletta leaned forward. "He only wants you, DeeDee."

More tears blurred DeeDee's vision, but she blinked them away. "You can't know that."

"Oh, but I do." Carletta smiled. "I know my brother better than anyone in the world. From the first time he laid eyes on you, he changed. He's happier, more content, more trusting, and ready to open his heart to his one true mate. Please consider forgiving him, DeeDee. He's been miserable without you. If you feel for him even half of what he feels for you, please go to him and tell him. I'm not sure he'll make it anymore without you."

There was no keeping the tears at bay any longer after that. They streamed down her cheeks as she stared at the letter in her hands. By taking responsibility for the marriage not going, Caine had risked being ostracized from the pack, because the rule was that anyone who refused an arranged marriage could be ostracized. He'd done this for *her*. In case she didn't want to marry him, so that she wouldn't be punished. Caine MacPherson loved her. He really, truly loved her. And against all odds, against all the crazy reasons why she shouldn't, DeeDee loved him too. With all her heart and soul.

"Where is he?" she asked, pushing to her stockinged feet.

"He's going to the Promising Tree tonight." Carletta stood too. "Will you go too?"

"Absolutely." She pulled the other woman into a hug

then laughed. "I better tidy myself up first, though. This probably isn't the best look to meet my new mate, huh?"

Carletta pulled away and looked DeeDee up and down. "Maybe not, but I don't think Caine would mind at all." She tugged her from the room. "C'mon. I'll help you get ready."

CHAPTER 26

*C*aine stood beneath the gnarled pine tree in his wolf form, his thick fur keeping the bitter cold away. He'd run for miles and miles, trying to burn the memory of what had happened at The Tribunal from his mind, but nothing worked. Now, panting, he stood alone in the spot where couples came to confess their true love to their fated mates.

Man, I'm such a screwup.

With a whimper, wolf Caine lay down atop the snow and covered his muzzle with his front paws. Flakes shimmered in the air, falling softly all around him, clinging to his fur and face. Stars twinkled brightly in the plush black sky, and through the thick forest, glimmers of the warm holiday lights flickered from the village of Silver Hollow beyond.

The whole scene was magical.

Too bad he'd lost his one shot to be with the true love of his life.

He rolled onto his side, burying his nose in the snow, running through all the mistakes he'd made with DeeDee in his mind. Why hadn't he been honest with her from the start? Why had he kept his identity hidden when telling her the truth would've been so much simpler?

Because he was scared, that was why. Carletta had been right, as always. Scared of getting hurt again, scared of losing his heart to a woman who might only want him for who he was, not for what he was inside. Never mind the fact DeeDee had been nothing like Brenda.

DeeDee was kind and sweet and loyal. She loved embroidery and made snarky remarks and got all his stupid jokes. Regret made his werewolf heart ache even more, if that were possible. He'd been wrong about her, so wrong. And now he'd blown any chance he'd had of making her his forever.

Huffing, he rolled onto his back and stared up at the stars through the bare branches of the Promising Tree. If only he'd realized what an amazing bond they'd shared. If only he'd opened himself up to her and let her inside. If only...

Each time Caine closed his eyes, he felt their connection pulsing strongly inside him. Her thoughts were his thoughts now, and vice versa. Her emotions too flowed through their connection. Nothing would change that, he knew, even though she wanted nothing to do with him. So he'd live the rest of his life with the woman he loved more than life itself in his head and in his heart, even as she moved on and found a new mate. And that would most likely kill him. Just the thought of another man, another wolf, touching her, holding her, making her laugh and cry and love, made him want to tear something limb from limb.

Mainly himself, for being such an idiot.

As if conjured from his imagination, soft footfalls vibrated through the ground beneath him, and Caine rolled over to see another werewolf approaching through the trees, a female, more beautiful than any wolf he'd ever seen.

DeeDee.

Mine.

His wolf stood at attention, ears perked and eyes watchful as she stood before him in her wolf form. Man, she was gorgeous—all tawny auburn fur and sparkling whiskey-colored eyes. Flecks of gold streaked her mane, and a spark of anger still lit her gaze.

Wolf Caine lowered his head and sent her his thoughts telepathically. *"I was afraid you wouldn't come."*

At first she didn't respond, and Caine started to worry that perhaps she couldn't read his thoughts after all. Then she pawed at the snow, the edges of her muzzle twitching slightly with tension as she telegraphed her thoughts to him and confirmed that yes, she was his true, bonded soul mate. *"I almost didn't."*

Through their connection, her apprehension and anger throbbed. She was still mad at him for lying.

Understandable. But by some miracle, Caine had been given another chance, another shot to redeem himself, and he wasn't about to blow things again. He hesitantly stepped toward DeeDee, his tail down and his gaze still lowered, showing both his remorse and his lack of aggression. *"Please. Let me explain."*

Tense moments passed as she watched him. Then, finally, she tilted her head to the side and started around toward the more private back area of the Promising Tree, her thoughts giving him little ground. "Start talking."

"I NEVER MEANT to hurt you, DeeDee." His jumbled thoughts conveyed his obvious discomfort, and it nearly had her forgiving Caine on the spot. But she kept her reserve, wanting to make him suffer a bit longer. After all, he'd had her on pins and needles for weeks—literally, given his secret identity in the embroidery chat room. *"I wanted to tell you the truth from the beginning, but I was scared. I've been through a lot in my past and had my heart trampled. I realize that's no excuse for not being up front with you, but perhaps you can find it within yourself to forgive me."*

She exhaled slowly, staring out across the snowy landscape. She'd run all the way here from her house, hoping to burn off some of the excess energy boiling inside her. No luck. Her system was still flooded with emotions and adrenaline, making her jumpy. Not to mention the fact she still couldn't get that letter Carletta had shown her off her mind. Caine had given her an out, even back then. He never would've forced her into a loveless marriage. That counted for a lot in her book, though lingering hurt still ached in her chest. *"I wish you'd at least given me a chance,"* she said to him through her thoughts, *"instead of lumping me in with all those other women from your past."*

He gave a short snort, shaking himself all over, his thick tawny-blond fur shimmering beneath the full moon's light. *"Correction. A woman. Brenda. That's it. My playboy reputation is exaggerated."* He hung his head again. *"And you're right. I should have given you an opportunity to make the decision on your own. It's just that people always have these preconceived ideas about me based on my family and my standing in my pack. When I saw you that first day, sitting with your friends at the juice bar, laughing and carefree, I assumed you'd be the same."*

"Wait." She stilled. *"You remember me from that day at the juice bar?"*

"Of course." His amber eyes met hers, the spark of heat in them sending a shiver of warmth through her. *"I remember every single time I've seen you, DeeDee. Not to mention all our conversations in the chat room. Those were my favorite."*

Mine too.

She swallowed hard against the constriction blocking her throat and batted around a pinecone with her paw. *"We did have some good conversations."*

"Yes, we did. No one makes a French knot like you."

The edges of DeeDee's muzzle twitched up into the equivalent of a wolfish smile. *"Not tonight, I don't. Since our argument, I haven't been able to even get a simple straight stitch right. Had to rip out a whole section tonight and start over again."*

"No," he said, looking up at her, hope in his gaze. *"Your work's always impeccable."*

She stepped a tad closer to him. *"That day, at your house, I was in awe of those framed pieces on your walls. If I'm the queen of cross-stitch, then you are definitely the king of embroidery."*

"That's sweet of you to say." He inched closer still. *"You don't think it's unmanly for me to continue my hobby?"*

"With your skill? No way." She nosed the pinecone she'd been playing with his way, going down on her front legs with her rump in the air, encouraging him to play. *"I think it shows an immense amount of patience and attention to detail. Not to mention creativity. Besides, who cares what your hobbies are if they don't hurt anyone else and you enjoy them?"*

"Yeah?" He batted the pinecone with his paw, sending it skittering across the top of the snow. Caine glanced at her, that playful glint back in his gorgeous amber eyes.

"Oh yeah." She took off for their toy at the same time he did, and they ended up tumbling together through the snow, each wolf grappling for the pinecone, giving gentle nips and swats at the other.

At last, panting and tired, they stopped the chase and returned to the Promising Tree. Both lay down beneath the tall pine, their front paws touching and their muzzles inches away from each other.

For DeeDee, there was no question Caine was her soul mate, her one true love.

"I really am sorry," he said telepathically at last. *"Do you think you can forgive me?"*

She watched him, wanting to tell him yes but having too much fun toying with her new mate to let him off the hook so easily. *"Maybe. If you promise to show me how you get that amazing shading in your embroidery."*

Caine looked surprised before he hid it behind a mask of cool. *"I can't give away all my secrets."*

"You better, mate," she replied. *"No more secrets between us. Period."*

Slowly, he crept forward on his belly, until his furry face nuzzled hers, all his love and care and affection flooding through their connection to fill her heart to bursting.

Caine snuffled into her ear. *"Did you just call me your mate?"*

"I did." She nipped at the side of his muzzle then licked the spot tenderly. *"If you still want me."*

"If I still want you?" Caine pushed to his feet then rose on his back legs, claws slashing as he carved deep grooves into the bark of the Promising Tree. *"DeeDee Clawson, will you marry me?"*

Eyes stinging with tears, she rose on wobbly legs and placed her claw marks across his, sealing their hearts and their fates together. *"Yes, Caine Hunter MacPherson. I will."*

EPILOGUE

hree Days Later…

"So if you want this section here slightly darker than the part next to it, you take the stitch under, then around, then over and through, like this." DeeDee watched Caine's expert fingers work the embroidery thread through a difficult section of her appaloosa piece with ease. Sewing wasn't the only thing his talented hands were good at, either. She snuggled in closer and kissed his cheek. "That's amazing. You're amazing."

"No, my lass. You are." He gently kissed her lips, then her jaw, then her ear. "I'm glad you're here with me on Christmas Eve."

"Me too." She cuddled her face into his neck and sighed happily. "When will the others arrive?"

A knock echoed from the front door, as if on cue.

Caine chuckled, setting the embroidery aside before

kissing DeeDee again then pushing to his feet. "Sounds like they're outside now."

She watched him walk out of their secret craft room, all masculine grace and confidence. A moment later, voices echoed from the grand living room—all four Quinn cousins plus Dex. They'd invited them over to thank them for their help that night at the Tribunal and to celebrate the holidays. Plus, the huge house seemed empty with just the two of them since Carletta had flown back out to Hollywood to celebrate Christmas with her West Coast friends.

DeeDee stood and straightened her outfit—a funky Christmas sweater with a large wolf wearing a jingly Santa hat on the front, identical to the one Caine wore—then headed out into the kitchen, careful to lock the craft room door behind her. She loved embroidery and had urged Caine to go public with his hobby, but he still wanted to keep it a secret, so she honored his wishes. Maybe one day she'd get him to come out of his craft closet.

Snorting at her own wit, DeeDee stepped into the great room in time to greet their new arrivals. She hugged each of the Quinns and took their coats then offered them homemade eggnog. It seemed the Quinns had all brought their familiars with them too—Issy's adorable little Pomeranian, Bella; Ember's fluffy little puffball kittens, Bellatrix and Endora; Gray's squawking cockatoo, Cosmo; and Raine's ever-growing Venus flytrap, Mortimer. Even Brimstone deigned to grace

Caine's estate with his presence. The large charcoal-gray cat strutted in, taking a good look around before draping himself across the slate hearth in front of the crackling fire. He gave DeeDee a superior look with his hellfire-orange gaze and purred loudly.

She glanced at Issy, who shook her head. "He says you may bring him a bowl of cream. I say he can drink eggnog like the rest of us if he's thirsty."

Brimstone gave a dismissive swipe of his tail then turned away to groom his paws.

"I'll see what I can find." DeeDee snorted.

Once everyone was settled, eggnog in hand, DeeDee took a seat on the sofa beside Caine and snuggled into his side. She'd never been one for overt displays of affection in public and had teased Dex relentlessly about holding hands or kissing Issy when they were out together. Now, though, she couldn't seem to stop touching Caine. His warmth penetrated through her sweater and seeped into her skin, making her feel safe and secure and infinitely cared for. She couldn't get enough, would never get enough of her mate.

My mate.

The words still seemed strange sometimes. Then their connection would tug around her heart, and she'd fall right back into place beside him, where she belonged.

Raine set Morty's pot down on the coffee table, and DeeDee couldn't help eyeing the plant suspiciously. "You didn't bring him to spy on us, did you?"

"Don't be silly." Raine took a large sip of her eggnog.

"I felt bad leaving him home alone on Christmas Eve. You should open your gifts."

"Gifts?" DeeDee asked.

"Look," Caine said, pointing to a small pile of beautifully wrapped presents under the tree against the wall.

"Where did those come from?" she asked. They hadn't been there earlier.

"We each brought you something to celebrate your engagement," Gray said, smiling. There was still a lingering hint of sadness in his aqua gaze, and DeeDee's heart pinched for him. She knew that look well, had felt the emotion many times herself before she'd found her mate.

Loneliness.

Gray was an excellent hairdresser and witch, and an even better friend. He deserved love and happiness too. Perhaps her and Caine marking the Promising Tree and declaring their true love would fulfill another of the tree's legends—that they could pass on the gift of finding true love to another. If so, then she wished it for her friend Gray Quinn. Without the whole murder-investigation-dead-body part, of course.

Caine stood and held out his hand to DeeDee. She took it, and together they walked over to the tree and took a seat on the floor.

"This was so thoughtful of all of you," Caine said.

"That's what friends do," Issy said, lacing her fingers through Dex's.

"Besides, you haven't opened them yet," Dex said. "Maybe you won't like them."

"I'm sure we will, buddy," DeeDee said, smiling at him. "Thanks."

"No problem." Dex kissed the back of Issy's hand then grinned.

Caine opened a small box covered in shiny silver paper first. Inside was a golden pair of specially designed fur-trimming scissors from Gray. He held them out for DeeDee to inspect.

"Oh, these are lovely! Thanks so much," she said.

"For when you can't make it into Sheer Magic," Gray said with a wink.

"Right." Him casting that beauty spell on her all those months ago had started DeeDee's journey to true love. She'd never be able to thank him enough. "I'll still keep my regular appointments, though. Don't worry."

Next was a box of delicious chocolates from Ember. Her shop, Divine Cravings, had the most delectable candy in the state of New Hampshire. DeeDee also knew sometimes Ember and her cousins liked to put little charms and hexes on the chocolates, so when Caine took one and prepared to pop it in his mouth, she stopped him.

"These are...*normal* chocolate, right?" she asked Ember, giving her a wary look.

"Oh yes." Ember smiled, her long auburn hair looking festive with sprigs of holly attached to her headband. "Just chocolate and caramel and tons of love. Promise."

"Okay." DeeDee took one too and ate it along with Caine. The salty caramel and pecans were the perfect foil to the rich dark chocolate. Turtles were her favorites, and she was touched Ember remembered. "Thank you."

"Always welcome," Ember said, blowing them both a kiss. "Blessings on your engagement and marriage."

The last gift was a bit larger and had a tag on top stating it was from Issy and Dex. DeeDee raised a brow at her detective partner, and he just shrugged.

"Sorry," Dex said. "No hints from me. Issy picked it out from her shop and wrapped it before I saw what was inside."

Two extra-large, thick leather dog collars, as it turned out, were what was inside the box. DeeDee picked up the red one, its sliver spikes glinting in the lights from the tree, and gave Caine an inquiring stare. "Is there something you're not telling me?"

He laughed and kissed her quickly. "We'll talk about it later."

"Aw, man," Dex said, shaking his head. "I don't even want to know what you two are going to do with those things."

Laughter filled the room, and DeeDee carefully packed all their new gifts away and put them back under the tree before joining Caine on the sofa. "Thanks again, everyone. Those gifts are so wonderful. We really appreciate them."

"Especially the collars," Caine said, waggling his brows.

DeeDee smacked him on the arm then kissed his cheek. "Don't pay any attention to my mate, Issy. His mind's in the gutter lately."

"Oh, I think it's wonderful you two found each other at last," Issy said, grinning. "I'm a sucker for unconventional love stories."

"Can't get any more unconventional than a murder investigation," Raine said.

"Truth," DeeDee said. "You know, I almost feel sorry for the two women arrested. After all, poor Laura and Gina had to put up with Tucker Rockwood all that time, and honestly, he was kind of a jerk."

Caine's phone buzzed, and he pulled it from his pocket then chuckled. "My sister, Carletta, wishes us all a Merry Christmas."

He held out the screen to show them all the picture she'd sent— Carletta and friends sitting on the beach, enjoying cocktails in the sunshine. The temperatures outside in Silver Hollow were a balmy fifteen degrees, and it had been snowing steadily since that morning. Most likely, they'd end up with a foot or more on the ground before it was all over.

DeeDee laughed and took the phone from Caine to type in a quick response. In the past few days, she and Caine's sister had spent a lot more time together and had become, if not good friends quite yet, then at least fond of each other. She now realized Carletta's somewhat antagonistic ways were to protect her brother from more heartache, and DeeDee understood her motives.

"Hey," Issy said, snuggling closer into Dex's side. "Have you guys seen that gnarly old pine tree in the forest? Dex and I pass it almost every day when we go out snowshoeing. The thing has looked half dead for months, but now it's filled with fresh new greenery. Strangest thing ever. Must be the magic of Christmas."

Caine and DeeDee exchanged a look, then a kiss, laughing.

"Yeah," she said, rubbing noses with him. "The magic of Christmas."

The doorbell rang again, causing DeeDee to jump. "That must be Stan."

Dex frowned at her. "You invited Stan?"

DeeDee shrugged. "Just for one drink. His shift is over and it *is* Christmas eve."

Stan had volunteered to take the holiday shift since he didn't have family in the area. That way, DeeDee, Dex, and Owen could spend time at home. It was decent of the guy, considering he wasn't usually that nice. Maybe being under the influence of Ursula would be a good thing even if it did make him act spacey and unpredictable.

"I'll get it," Caine said, pushing to his feet once more. "I'm regretting letting Jarvis have the night off, though."

DeeDee knew better. Their butler was like another member of their family, and no way would Caine let the guy be separated from his loved ones over the holidays. In fact, he'd not only given the guy Christmas Eve off with pay, he'd given him the entire week between

Christmas and New Year's Day off as well. And supplied him with a tidy bonus as a gift.

Caine stepped back to allow a somewhat agitated Stan inside. He rushed into the living room where everyone was sitting.

"Hey, buddy. What's wrong?" Dex handed him an eggnog. "Something happening down at the station?"

Stan sniffled then scratched at the marks Ursula had left on his neck. They still weren't healed, from what DeeDee could see. He wriggled inside his suit then scowled. "Nothing's going on at all at the station, but I've been doing a little more digging into the Rockwood case while I'm still here."

"Aren't you heading back to the home office soon?" Dex asked, giving DeeDee an eager glance.

"Early tomorrow. I won't see either of you before I leave. That's one of the reasons I came over." Stan sipped the eggnog thoughtfully. "The other reason is that one thing is still niggling at me about this whole murder mess. Gina Presti claimed there was a giant werewolf that busted down the door of her trailer and held her until the police arrived. She says it's what broke up the fight between her and Deputy Clawson." He turned to DeeDee. "But I didn't see anything about it in your report, Deputy."

Stunned, she opened her mouth to respond then closed it. Caine tensed beside her. She'd hoped that whole thing would just fall through the cracks, unnoticed.

"Oh...well," Dex said, coming to her aid, "I wouldn't put much stock in what Gina Presti claims she saw. After all, she lied to get away with murdering Tucker Rockwood. Who's to say she isn't lying about seeing this wolf too?"

"Hmm." Stan shrugged, that slightly dazed look coming over his features again. "Yeah, I guess you're right. Imagine paranormals here in the nice town of Silver Hollow. Ha!"

"Yeah, imagine," Dex and DeeDee echoed.

Stan chugged down the rest of the eggnog then handed the empty glass to Dex. "Thanks for inviting me for the drink. I gotta go pack." Stan shuffled out the door, then turned to face them one last time, halfway out onto the porch. "I'll be back in a few weeks to check in again. Call me crazy, but I sense there's more under the surface here in Silver Hollow. Oh, and keep an eye on that medical examiner, Ursula. There's something...*odd* about her. Who knows? Maybe I'll have to move here myself one day to investigate."

The front door closed behind him, and everyone burst into laughter. Given how mesmerized Stan had been the last week or so, under Ursula's thrall, he couldn't find his butt with both hands. Though DeeDee suspected time and distance would change that. The further he was from Ursula the more the influence of her bite would wear off. She'd have to be on guard when good old Stan returned. For now, though, she had the holidays to celebrate and a new husband to love and adore.

While the others talked amongst themselves, DeeDee nuzzled her face into Caine's neck, happier than she could ever remember being. "I love you, Caine MacPherson," she whispered against his skin.

Caine cupped her cheek, forcing her to meet his gaze. "I love you too, my lass."

Her mate's kisses and love were the best gifts DeeDee ever received.

****

Sign up for my VIP reader list and get my books at the lowest discount price:
http://www.leighanndobbs.com/newsletter

Join my Facebook Readers group and get special content and the inside scoop on my books:
https://www.facebook.com/groups/ldobbsreaders

More Books in the Silver Hollow Series:
A Spell of Trouble (Book 1)
Spell Disaster (Book 2)
Nothing To Croak About (Book 3)

If you want to receive a text message on your cell phone for new releases, text COZYMYSTERY to 88202 (sorry, this only works for US cell phones!)

Fatal Fortune

Mooseamuck Island Cozy Mystery Series

* * *

A Zen For Murder

A Crabby Killer

A Treacherous Treasure

Mystic Notch

Cat Cozy Mystery Series

* * *

Ghostly Paws

A Spirited Tail

A Mew To A Kill

Paws and Effect

Probable Paws

Lexy Baker Cozy Mystery Series

* * *

Lexy Baker Cozy Mystery Series Boxed Set Vol 1 (Books 1-4)

Or buy the books separately:

Killer Cupcakes

Dying For Danish

Murder, Money and Marzipan

3 Bodies and a Biscotti

Brownies, Bodies & Bad Guys

Bake, Battle & Roll

Wedded Blintz

Scones, Skulls & Scams

Ice Cream Murder

Mummified Meringues

Brutal Brulee (Novella)

No Scone Unturned

Magical Romance with a Touch of Mystery

***

Something Magical

Curiously Enchanted

Romantic Comedy

***

Corporate Chaos Series

In Over Her Head (book 1)

Contemporary Romance

***

Reluctant Romance

Sweet Romance (Written As Annie Dobbs)

Hometown Hearts Series

***

No Getting Over You (Book 1)

***

Sweetrock Sweet and Spicy Cowboy Romance

Some Like It Hot

Too Close For Comfort

Regency Romance

* * *

Scandals and Spies Series:

Kissing The Enemy

Deceiving the Duke

Tempting the Rival

Charming the Spy

Pursuing the Traitor

The Unexpected Series:

An Unexpected Proposal

An Unexpected Passion

Dobbs Fancytales:

Dobbs Fancytales Boxed Set Collection

———

Western Historical Romance

***

Goldwater Creek Mail Order Brides:

Faith

American Mail Order Brides Series:

Chevonne: Bride of Oklahoma

———————————

ROMANTIC SUSPENSE

WRITING AS LEE ANNE JONES:

* * *

The Rockford Security Series:

ABOUT THE AUTHOR

USA Today Bestselling author Leighann Dobbs has had a passion for reading since she was old enough to hold a book, but she didn't put pen to paper until much later in life. After a twenty-year career as a software engineer with a few side trips into selling antiques and making jewelry, she realized you can't make a living reading books, so she tried her hand at writing them and discovered she had a passion for that, too! She lives in New Hampshire with her husband, Bruce, their trusty Chihuahua mix, Mojo, and beautiful rescue cat, Kitty.

Her book "Dead Wrong" won the "Best Mystery Romance" award at the 2014 Indie Romance Convention.

Her book "Ghostly Paws" was the 2015 Chanticleer Mystery & Mayhem First Place category winner in the Animal Mystery category.

Don't miss out on the early buyers discount on Leighann's next cozy mystery - signup for email notifications:

http://www.leighanndobbs.com/newsletter

Want text alerts for new releases? TEXT alert straight on your cellphone. Just text COZYMYSTERY to 88202
(sorry, this only works for US cell phones!)

Connect with Leighann on Facebook:
http://facebook.com/leighanndobbsbooks

Join her VIP Readers group on Facebook:
https://www.facebook.com/groups/ldobbsreaders

This is a work of fiction.

None of it is real. All names, places, and events are products of the author's imagination. Any resemblance to real names, places, or events are purely coincidental, and should not be construed as being real.